Hurricane Season Hustle

Reviewers Love the Scotty Bradley Series

Royal Street Reveillon

"Herren's wit, ingenuity, and sharp social eye are a constant delight, and every time I read him I fall in love with New Orleans all over again. Scotty may have hung up his go-go boots, but I hope his adventures go on and on."—Alex Marwood, Edgar and Macavity Award–winning author of *The Wicked Girls* and *The Darkest Secret*

"A delicious, witty, deftly plotted mystery. Greg Herren offers up a compulsively readable tale."—Megan Abbott, Edgar-winning author of *Queenpin* and *Dare Me*

"What a treat to be able to read a brand-new book from Greg Herren featuring one of my favorite sleuths, Scotty Bradley…5 out of 5 for this favorite gay mystery series." —P*hilip Bahr, Librarian, Fairfield Public Library*

"[A] witty, engrossing slice of New Orleans life (and death)…delicious bits of gossip and hints of hushed-up scandal…wry observations about old money in the new New Orleans…a plot full of lively characters and satisfying twists."—*Lia Matera, author of the Willa Jansson and Laura Di Palma series*

Baton Rouge Bingo

"I very much enjoyed this book. I love the way Mr. Herren writes, and the humor that he pops into the story from time to time…It is a pure and simple mystery, and I loved it…I recommend this book to anyone liking a good mystery with gay MCs."—*Love Bytes: Same Sex Book Reviews*

Lambda Literary Award Finalist *Vieux Carré Voodoo*

"Herren's packed plot, as always in this imaginative series… revels in odd twists and comic turns; for example, the third man of the ménage returns, revealed as a James Bond type. It all makes for a roller-coaster caper."—Richard Labonte, *Book Marks*

"This novel confirms that out of the many New Orleans mystery writers, Greg Herren is indeed one to watch." —*Reviewing the Evidence*

"[T]his was well worth waiting for. Herren has a knack for developing colorful primary and supporting characters the reader actually cares about, and involving them in realistic, though extreme, situations that make his books riveting to the mystery purist. Bravo, and five gumbo-stained stars out of five."—*Echo Magazine*

"Herren's work is drenched in the essence of the Big Easy, the city's geography even playing a large part in the solution of a riddle at whose end lies the aforementioned Eye of Kali. But unlike the city, it is not languid. Herren hits the ground running and only lets up for two extremely interesting dream sequences, the latter of which is truly chilling. Is this a breezy beach read? Maybe, but it has far more substance than many. You can spend a few sunny, sandy afternoons with this resting on your chest and still feel as if you've read a book. But even if you're not at the beach, Herren's work makes great backyard or rooftop reading, and this one is a terrific place to start."—*Out In Print*

Praise for Greg Herren

Sleeping Angel "will probably be put on the young adult (YA) shelf, but the fact is that it's a cracking good mystery that general readers will enjoy as well. It just happens to be about teens…A unique viewpoint, a solid mystery and good characterization all conspire to make *Sleeping Angel* a welcome addition to any shelf, no matter where the bookstores stock it."—Jerry Wheeler, *Out in Print*

"This fast-paced mystery is skillfully crafted. Red herrings abound and will keep readers on their toes until the very end. Before the accident, few readers would care about Eric, but his loss of memory gives him a chance to experience dramatic growth, and the end result is a sympathetic character embroiled in a dangerous quest for truth." —*VOYA*

"Herren, a loyal New Orleans resident, paints a brilliant portrait of the recovering city, including insights into its tight-knit gay community. This latest installment in a powerful series is sure to delight old fans and attract new ones."—*Publishers Weekly*

"Fast-moving and entertaining, evoking the Quarter and its gay scene in a sweet, funny, action-packed way."—*New Orleans Times-Picayune*

"Herren does a fine job of moving the story along, deftly juggling the murder investigation and the intricate relationships while maintaining several running subjects."—*Echo Magazine*

"An entertaining read."—*OutSmart Magazine*

"A pleasant addition to your beach bag."—*Bay Windows*

"Greg Herren gives readers a tantalizing glimpse of New Orleans." —*The Midwest Book Review*

"Herren's characters, dialogue and setting make the book seem absolutely real."—*The Houston Voice*

"So much fun it should be thrown from Mardi Gras floats!"—*New Orleans Times-Picayune*

"Greg Herren just keeps getting better."—*Lambda Book Report*

By the Author

The Scotty Bradley Adventures

Bourbon Street Blues

Jackson Square Jazz

Mardi Gras Mambo

Vieux Carré Voodoo

Who Dat Whodunnit

Baton Rouge Bingo

Garden District Gothic

Royal Street Reveillon

Mississippi River Mischief

Hurricane Season Hustle

The Chanse MacLeod Mysteries

Murder in the Rue Dauphine

Murder in the Rue St. Ann

Murder in the Rue Chartres

Murder in the Rue Ursulines

Murder in the Garden District

Murder in the Irish Channel

Murder in the Arts District

Young Adult

Sleeping Angel

Sara

Lake Thirteen

New Adult

Timothy

The Orion Mask

Dark Tide

Survivor's Guilt and Other Stories

Going Down for the Count
(Writing as Cage Thunder)

Wicked Frat Boy Ways
(Writing as Todd Gregory)

Edited with J.M. Redmann

Women of the Mean Streets: Lesbian Noir

Men of the Mean Streets: Gay Noir

Night Shadows: Queer Horror

Edited as Todd Gregory

Rough Trade

Sweat

Anything for a Dollar

Blood Sacraments

Hurricane Season Hustle

by

Greg Herren

2026

HURRICANE SEASON HUSTLE

ISBN 13: 978-1-63679-882-0

This Trade Paperback Original Is Published By
Bold Strokes Books, Inc.
P.O. Box 249
Valley Falls, NY 12185

First Edition: February 2026

Credits
Editor: Ruth Sternglantz
Production Design: Stacia Seaman
Cover Design by Tammy Seidick

This is for CYNDI HILL—thank you for your patience!

Prologue

American vanities come to dust in New Orleans. On the August night in 2019 when Hurricane Hester formed in the Gulf of Mexico a mere day after the system formed off the coast of the Yucatán and started moving north slowly, forces were already in play in New Orleans which would have made the upcoming weekend a challenge at best without the weather complication. One of the difficulties of having a mid-August birthday, besides the crippling heat and humidity, is that it's the height of hurricane season, which lasts through September. So many storms, so many memories.

The history of New Orleans is littered with horrific storms. The French settlement on a high rise along the Father of Waters was obliterated by one such occurrence within ten years of its founding. The French waited for the floodwater to go down, cleaned up, and started over again, which became the dominant pattern of New Orleans history, rinsed and repeated time after time for over three hundred years. There have been monsters in the past, like the great hurricane of 1915, which wiped out numerous communities along the rims of the two big lakes bordered on the city.

And of course, everyone remembers Katrina fourteen years ago.

Fourteen years have somehow passed since that incredibly dark time for New Orleans. White hairs have started showing up in my buzzed short hair. The crow's-feet around my eyes look like eagles now. Muscles and joints ache and moan and groan, and muscle fatigue from the gym doesn't dissipate quickly the way it used to. The siren song of gay bars and the dance floor isn't impossible to ignore as it once was, and besides, hangovers last longer and seem more intense than they used to when I was younger. The bars are different than they used to be, too. Now, gay bars are filled with straight women (bachelorette parties are the worst), and the gay guys are all staring at their phones when they aren't on the dance floor—and some apparently have their phones grafted to their hands on the dance floor, too. I've resisted the urge to download the let's-fuck-now apps to my phone so far. Besides, I have a terrific sex life already, thank you very much.

I even turned forty a few years ago, and the world didn't end.

This certain summer was already a rough one for me—

Oh, wait, you may not know who I am. My name is Scotty Bradley, of the Uptown Bradleys and the Garden District Diderots. Despite that impressive society pedigree, I don't belong to any Mardi Gras krewes or fraternal organizations—although I could if I wanted to, despite being gay. That would have been a strike against me as recently as thirty years ago, unless I chose to remain closeted, as so many others before me did. My parents rebelled against all that society stuff their parents put them through when they were kids and remain committed to social and environmental justice to this day. They're what used to be called hippies, I think. I was lucky to be born to them. They love that I'm gay, belong to PFLAG, and march in Pride parades. They raised me—and my older siblings—to always question authority and to fight for the less privileged. My older brother Storm went to law school, and my sister Rain is married to a surgeon. She's a lady who lunches, and while she can be as radical as my parents, she *likes* the society stuff and is proud to be in the Krewe of Iris.

How is my name Scotty when they have such unique names? Scotty is my middle name. Both sides of the family apparently demanded that Mom and Dad give me a more traditional family name, so they gave me my grandmothers' maiden names: Milton Scott. Yes, they named me Milton Bradley. Storm started calling me Scotty when we were kids, and now hardly anyone remembers what my actual first name is.

Besides the DMV, the IRS, insurance companies, and the passport office.

I've considered dropping the Milton legally, or switching it to Scott Milton, but never got around to it.

Which tells me it doesn't matter that much to me anyway.

I also have two life partners, Frank Sobieski and Colin Cioni. I met the two of them the year before Katrina, that last Southern Decadence weekend of the *before* times. Frank was a Special Agent for the FBI, Colin was using cat burglar as his cover story for the weekend, and we all kind of fell in love with each other. Those first couple of years were rough. There were a lot of layers to peel back with Colin, as it turned out—he worked for an international guns-for-hire organization called Blackledge. We knew he'd been trained by the Mossad when he was young, but he left the Mossad in his mid-to-late twenties. For several years, he let us believe he was a murderer.

I mean, he let us think he'd killed two of my half uncles. (It's a *loooong* story.) But he finally was able to tell us the truth, and we've lived happily ever after ever since.

Well, we would have if not for my bad habit of stumbling over dead bodies.

Our most recent dead body case brought up something from my past—far back, when I was a kid—and forced me to recognize that the way I'd always remembered that something was not, in fact, correct and was much worse than I ever believed it to be. I mean, finding out that your first love was actually a pedophile and a groomer would be a shock to most people. Colin and Frank thought it might not be a bad idea to see a therapist, work through it with a professional.

I didn't know what to expect from therapy. I've always been happy-go-lucky, someone who always tries to see the positive in everything. My motto has always been *Life doesn't give you anything you can't handle—it's how you handle it that matters.*

That has always done well for me.

But even I was having trouble seeing the positive in being groomed as a teenager.

There was also a lot of stuff I couldn't share with my therapist. I couldn't tell Dr. Gargaro about Colin's job, or the dead Russian I came home to just before last Christmas. I also couldn't tell Dr. Gargaro that I had a psychic gift that doesn't always work and that I don't completely understand. I couldn't tell him that I read tarot cards so the universe could speak to me, that I'd once communed with a ghost, or that sometimes I go to another plane where I speak to the Goddess—and I have no idea who the Goddess is or what she represents.

Yeah, that would land me in a psych ward with no chance of getting out, wouldn't it?

But there was enough stuff with my wrestling coach to get through before I had to worry about sharing anything else beyond that.

We spent the summer of 2019 living on my Diderot grandparents' expansive property in the Garden District while our town house on Decatur Street was being renovated—and was almost finished. Cooper Construction was supposed to have had the house done so we could move back in by July 1, but *nothing* is ever on time in New Orleans. I was just glad we'd be able to move back home at the end of August. I stopped by earlier in the week to get an idea of the progress, and I had to admit the place looked amazing, even unfinished. I'd been living on that property since I was in my twenties, and I was grateful every day the family friends who'd owned it sold it to me when they retired and moved away. I was hesitant—the price they'd asked was high, though below market value—but if they sold it to someone else, we might have to move. My family was always telling me I needed to invest in property, so I bit the bullet. Colin, Frank, and I had worked with the architect to come up with plans for the redo of the entire inside, and turning the place from its old setup—commercial first floor, apartments on the three floors above—into a one-family house was sorely overdue.

The house *had* needed a glow-up for a while, and Storm said turning it into a single residence would at least double the value.

Whatever. I was never going to sell the place. Investments and that sort of thing don't interest me. It's too much like gambling, only with enormous sums of money. I know how precious money can be. I'd been cut off from my trust fund after I flunked out of college and barely scratched out a living in my twenties as a personal trainer and occasional stripper. This was both sets of grandparents trying to get me to learn the value of a dollar, or something like that. I just wanted a safe, secure place for my little family to call home.

Frank's nephew Taylor also lives with us. His homophobic evangelical parents threw him out when he came out to them, and he came to live with us. Having him around has been an education, and make no mistake, I would kill to protect him. Nobody fucks with my guys.

Anyway, we moved into the old carriage house on my grandparents' property. The first floor of the building is now storage—it's very jumbled and cluttered down there, and very dusty. The second floor was the old chauffeur's apartment, back when someone was on salary. Taylor moved into the main house, rather than with us. I'd hoped we'd be able to use the dower house, which was behind the main house, past the pool, but my annoying aunt Erica was staying there while recovering from a broken hip.

By the week before my birthday, I was more than ready to move home.

And then another hurricane formed in the Gulf.

Chapter One

Ace of Pentacles, Reversed

Comfortable conditions are not an advantage

I began waking up to the pitter-patter of rain hitting the roof. Groggily I wondered if the streets were flooding, and if this was an outer band of the storm in the Gulf.

It had rained almost every day for nearly two weeks. Some of those storms brought a lot of rain in a short time, which always caused temporary street flooding around the city while the pumping stations tried to catch up. Weather forecasters were nervous about all the potential rain from this new storm since the ground was already saturated.

Hester had come up very quickly. Just two days ago, she was a disorganized system just off the Yucatán that no one outside the Hurricane Center was paying much attention to. The local news had mentioned it on their Wednesday night shows, and I felt a bit of a mental tug. My psychic gift didn't always work with storms—it said nothing about Katrina to me—but that pang of anxiety made me nervous. It had still been a tropical storm when I'd gone to bed last night but was heading straight for New Orleans and estimated to hit land this morning. The water in the Gulf was very warm, more than warm enough for rapid intensification. No one could agree how strong Hester would be by the time she came through New Orleans, but the range was Category 1 to 4. That wasn't reassuring. The storm had come up so fast we hadn't had a chance to even consider evacuating, so we were staying and riding it out here.

Which was not one of my favorite things to do in New Orleans.

We'd evacuated for every hurricane since Katrina.

I looked over at my alarm in the gray darkness and saw the glowing red numbers: 7:02. It was way too early to be awake on a Saturday…but *hurricane*.

But the bed felt warm and comfortable. Colin's body was warm and cuddly like always, too.

I moved closer to the warmth radiating from Colin's back. He sighed in his sleep, shifting a bit so he was pressed back against my body. I slipped my left arm over his back and curled it around his torso. Colin was always warm, and Frank jokingly called him our space heater. He felt great when it was cold in the winter. And despite the absence of any body fat, his skin was as soft as a baby's—except for his scars. For me, the scars only added to his sexiness, the contrast of the scars from years of working as a black ops agent. His job used to take him all over the world and away from us for months at a time. We'd gotten used to him showing up out of the blue over the years. We never knew where he was or what he was doing when he was away, which he would shamefacedly admit made him glad. But he'd quit when someone from that shadowy, dangerous world had followed him home to New Orleans and put us all in danger. It was nice having him home permanently.

Not, of course, that we were in our own house.

This storm was most likely one of Hester's outer bands. Last night The Weather Channel predicted the eye would pass over New Orleans in the late morning or early afternoon. I closed my eyes just as the house shook and the windows rattled from a loud clap of thunder.

How strong did she get overnight? I wondered, not really wanting to know. Dealing with the storm could wait, couldn't it? I didn't have to get up right away. Reality could be held at arm's length for a little while longer, right?

If only a mug of coffee would magically appear on the nightstand.

I burrowed closer in to Colin's back. The air-conditioning clicked on, and the rain was still playing musical scales on the roof. Was there anything more comforting than being warm and snug in bed while it rained?

That was when I realized Frank wasn't snoring softly on my other side.

I opened my eyes and lifted my head. No Frank.

Well, I wasn't falling back asleep *now*.

I disentangled my body from Colin gently, trying not to disturb him, and slid out from under the covers. It was cold in the apartment—we always kept it at meat locker temperatures—so I quickly pulled on my sweatpants and my ratty old LSU sweatshirt. I got up and stretched, looking around the big bedroom suite.

It was a great place, I reflected, but I'd rather be home.

Back in the days when my Diderot grandparents had a full-time chauffeur—I didn't ever remember them having one—the carriage house had an apartment on the second floor for him to live in. The Diderot limousine used to be parked on the first floor, and there was still an enormous garage door on the Chestnut Street side of the building. All the space down there was used for storage now—old furniture, boxes of books, all the makings of a great yard sale. No one had lived in the apartment for decades, but us moving in temporarily turned into a thing, which is how it usually went in the family. They refused to accept any rent money, and they wanted to pay for their cleaning team to come through. Frank felt uncomfortable *sponging off your grandparents*, as he put it, and the compromise we finally landed on was we'd pay for the cleaning crew and not pay rent.

And once I figured out what the going rate was for

apartments this size in the Garden District, I donated that amount to a shelter for people dealing with housing insecurity—and I still think I priced it too low.

It was a really nice place.

The apartment had both a front and a back staircase, but it was confusing as to which was which. Technically, the front stairs led down to a door that opened into my grandparents' side yard. What *I* considered the front was architecturally the back—the back of the carriage house was the side facing Chestnut Street. That always seemed, to me, like it should be the front. But…New Orleans. The back stairs were just past the primary suite's door. There was another bedroom on the other side of the hall, but we used that for a clothes closet because the one in the suite was tiny. The hallway ran between the bedrooms and opened out into a large living space. The kitchen was galley style, against the wall facing the yard, with a door on the right that led to the pantry and the front stairs.

The entire upstairs had hardwood floors and twelve-foot ceilings. Ceiling fans with chandeliers hung down in various spots throughout, but as for how the light switches worked? Well, let's just say someone had done an interesting job of wiring in the past.

Frank was standing at the Keurig, his back to me, waiting for his cup to finish brewing. I smiled. He was wearing an old, old pair of gray LSU sweatpants that really needed to be thrown away. The elasticity of the waistband was starting to give up, so they'd slid down to reveal the top of his hard ass and the start of the crack. I just stood there in the gloom for a few moments, drinking in his broad shoulders, muscular back, and that ridiculously tiny waist.

Who else wears 30 waist, 40 length pants? And isn't a teenager?

I moved silently across the floor and slid my arms around him from behind. He wasn't as warm as Colin, but his skin was firm and warm to the touch. I kissed him between his shoulder blades.

"I didn't wake you?" he asked as the machine sputtered and spat out the last gulp of his coffee. He turned around inside my arms and bent his neck to kiss the top of my head. Frank is almost six inches taller than me, at six two, but he's one of those people with an insanely high metabolism who struggles to put on bulk. He always has visible muscle striations, abs, and vascularity—and can eat whatever he wants whenever he wants as often as he wants.

I hate that about him. I *used* to be like that, but getting older has made it harder than it used to be.

Colin never gains an ounce anywhere, either, but he's an exercise fanatic. In his old line of work, he had to be.

I pressed my head against Frank's hard chest and listened to his heartbeat. "Nothing woke me, unless it was the rain. I didn't even know you'd gotten up," I replied, gliding my hands down his strong back, and cupped his solid buttocks in my hands. "How long have you been up?"

"I couldn't sleep," he replied. He kissed my forehead again, turning back to get his coffee. He got down another mug and brewed a cup for me. He's sweet like that. "Just lay there most of the night, staring at the ceiling." He shrugged. "Don't know why I couldn't sleep. I gave up about an hour ago and got up to see what's going on with the storm. I've been monitoring the weather and the news online since I got up. This rain started about an hour ago." He checked his Apple Watch as he said the words.

Frank hated hurricanes. I wasn't surprised he couldn't sleep the eve before one.

"So, is this Hester's outer bands?" I asked. I added a packet of sweetener and some French vanilla creamer in the mug as the coffee streamed down into it.

"Yeah, this is the first one to get to us." He took a sip

from his mug. "Right now, they're saying the eye is going to pass directly over Slidell. But the storm is starting to veer east more as it gets closer to shore." He gave me a look. "Jim Cantore is out in the East, by the Rigolets."

"Oh no." That wasn't good news. Jim Cantore was the hurricane guy from The Weather Channel, always reported from wherever the storm was likely to come, and was kind of a Hot Daddy. I'd sometimes watch storm coverage not affecting us, hoping the wind would blow his shirt off sometime.

Everyone joked that a hurricane wasn't real until Jim Cantore arrived.

The East was what everyone called New Orleans East, another part of the city created by filling in wetlands. It ran along the shore of Lake Pontchartrain on one side and Lake Borgne on the other, gradually narrowing to a slender spit of land at the Rigolets, the narrow pass connecting the two lakes together. "We're west of the eye?" I frowned. The west side of a hurricane was the dirty side—which meant more rain, higher winds, and possible tornadoes.

After two weeks of almost nonstop rain, the ground was already so saturated that the floodwater from the rains would just run off into the roads. The pumping system could never keep up with the kind of tropical rain we got here, let alone a forecast of eight to ten inches over the course of a few hours. The Garden District was one of the higher neighborhoods in the city—part of the *sliver by the river* that didn't flood after the failure of the federally built and maintained levees following Hurricane Katrina—and the gutters along the streets had been sunk several feet deep. There was a massive pothole on the next block downriver, the street pavement sinking so far that a cavern had opened between the sidewalk and the street. There was a gap of at least three inches between sidewalk and gutter, with the inevitable collapsing pavement around it.

We'd parked our Honda CR-V up behind the main house, in the little parking area on the other side of the main house. It was the highest spot on the property. Usually, we parked on Chestnut alongside the big garage door on that side of the carriage house. We moved it yesterday afternoon, just to be on the safe side.

Not that moving it to higher ground would protect it from flying debris or a falling tree, but you do what you can for preventive planning.

"She's a Category 3 now," Frank said grimly. "They called it shortly after I got up."

I froze as I felt the panic starting to rise. I caught my breath. Mom always said that panicking never did any good. My therapist had taught me some coping mechanisms, written some prescriptions. I refused to let the panic take over. Living in the tropics has drawbacks, and dealing with hurricanes is one of the big ones. Panic was a waste of energy, and we needed to reserve energy for dealing with the aftermath.

But I'd been hoping for better news on the strength front. All hurricanes were dangerous, but when it was Category 3 or higher, that was bad news. It's rare for a storm to strengthen so much once the evacuation window closed. Katrina spent some time in the Gulf as both a 5 and a 4 but came ashore as a 3. Everyone forgot the wind damage once the levees failed.

"I'm a bit worried," Frank replied. "We're going to get a lot of rain, and some major wind. The storm surge is going to be bad, too." He rubbed his eyes. "I hope it doesn't delay the renovation more."

"Don't say that," I replied, "or you'll manifest it." Frank had been deeply closeted most of the time he worked as a federal agent. He'd been raised in the same kind of Christianity that had tried warping Taylor's brain, so he still had some serious negative thinking problems. He wasn't as bad as he used to be, but his mind often reverted to the absolute worst-case scenario. It was his default.

Me? I couldn't imagine going through life expecting the worst just so I would never be disappointed.

It seemed so negative, you know?

I crossed myself. I wasn't Catholic but had spent my entire childhood trapped in Catholic schools. "Your mouth to the universe's ears," I replied, deciding not to fight the negative-thinking battle for now. "I like this place a lot, but I'm ready to be home." I plopped down on the overstuffed leather couch. Frank's laptop was open on the ugly glass-and-chrome coffee table, but it had gone to sleep. The screensaver was a great action shot—Frank in the ring with one of the masked guys. Kid Kaos? Something like that. He had a great body but… Frank's was better.

"So am I." Frank laughed. "It's not going to be easy getting Taylor to move back to Decatur Street," Frank said, sinking into the couch beside me and draping his leg over mine. "My socialist nephew certainly has taken to having servants and being waited on hand and foot."

"This is why the revolution is always doomed"—I grinned at him—"when even the most hardened revolutionary can be seduced by this opulent parasitic lifestyle, sucking the marrow out of the bones of the workers. I didn't expect him to go in on being a one-percenter once we got here."

Taylor Wheeler was in his final year at Tulane but was thinking about pursuing a master's. He'd blossomed since coming to live with us, having the freedom to finally be himself and not having to agree with us about everything. He had started moving farther to the left, all with the encouragement of my parents. I was getting used to the occasional lectures about my trust fund and the family fortunes, and every so often he'd say something that cut me to the quick.

I always wound up writing a big check to a charity after one of those lectures. Guilt money spends like every other kind, as Mom told me when I realized where the money in my trust had come from.

Which was why I never told Taylor where his tuition money came from, other than the trust.

And it wasn't a bad thing to recognize how much privilege you lived with.

We could have stayed in the main house—my grandparents' home was open and welcome for all of us whenever we needed for as long as we needed. The third floor was bedroom suites, and none were currently in use. Despite the Garden District homes-tour-showplace feel to the extravagant rooms on the first floor, the kitchen and the informal dining room were the only ones that got used a lot. Holiday gatherings and meals were in the big formal dining room, and there were always at least four Christmas trees in the windows visible from the street. Taylor's suite of rooms was on the second floor, on the opposite side from my grandparents' rooms. His was by the secret servant staircase that led from the kitchen to the fourth floor, so he could slip down for snacks whenever he needed one.

I hadn't even considered staying in the carriage house—mainly because I couldn't remember anyone ever living there, unlike the dower house, which was nestled against the back property line behind the main house, past the parking area and the swimming pool. The dower house had been built by the original Diderot who built the main house—his mother and his wife didn't get along, so he built his mother a home nearby. The dower house gets used regularly for guests, but alas, Aunt Erica showed no sign of moving out of there anytime soon. I kind of suspected she was drawing her convalescence out longer than was needed, but that was Aunt Erica.

Erica was recovering from a broken hip. She'd fallen getting out of a cab in the rain. She claimed she was sober as a judge. But it happened on a Friday afternoon, and Erica always drank her lunch at Galatoire's every Friday with friends. It didn't take Sherlock Holmes to figure out she'd been wasted and missed her footing in the rain. I visited her during her stay at Touro Infirmary but hadn't stayed long. She was her usual self, the room filled with balloons and flowers and plush toys, lording it over everyone from her hospital bed, loving every second of being the center of the attention. Mom said she was a textbook narcissist, and Aunt Erica had never done anything to disprove those words.

Aunt Erica had never been one of my favorite relatives—even when I was a child, she seemed a bit sour already. She was my mother's youngest sister. She'd been divorced four (or was it five?) times before giving up on marriage, but she also drank enough for people to talk about, not easy to do in a city whose social drinkers would be in rehab anywhere else. She'd made a lot of questionable choices in her life while being very critical of Mom's. Mom hated everything about New Orleans society and rejected it, becoming a counterculturalist progressive hippie living a very bohemian life with my father in the Quarter. Mom resisted doing any of the things well brought up young society ladies did in New Orleans—she didn't want to be a Mardi Gras maid or queen or anything, didn't enjoy attending balls, didn't want to make a debut or any of the archaic societal practices going back to before the Civil War, showing off women like prize cattle. She refused to go to Baylor or SMU for college, like all good Diderot girls—she went to UNO because she was already in love with Dad, and neither one of them wanted to leave New Orleans.

Totally understandable. I'd lived in Nashville for the sad two years I spent enrolled at Vanderbilt. I cried with joy every time I came home, until I flunked out.

Erica, on the other hand, grew up living the perfect New Orleans princess life, embracing all the things my mother abhorred. She did the dancing lessons, the piano lessons, and did all the prep work to grow into a proper New Orleans lady. She was the exact opposite of Mom in every way. She made her debut at eighteen, was first a maid and later Queen of Comus, Rex royalty being far too common and déclassé for the old-regime aristocratic Diderots. She went to SMU, where she met and married her first husband, an oil heir she divorced within a year. She moved back to New Orleans after that divorce and married her childhood sweetheart, a member of another family from the New Orleans nobility. That's the earliest husband of hers I remember. Despite spending her entire adolescence being the perfect daughter, she'd never supplanted Mom as the favorite. Mom said she became more bitter the older she got and started taking it out on the world. Mom was right about her being a narcissist—she always managed to make everything about her, she kept track of things as petty as birthday cards or who called who last, and could be downright cruel. She believed she should be everyone's top priority and got angry when she wasn't.

I rarely saw her, outside of command family performances. Mom had never been close to her, feeling sorrier for her than anything else. All I knew was she always smelled slightly of roses and whiskey. She'd had no children—although she treated her third husband's children from a previous marriage as her own, and of course, none of them could be bothered to help her out in her recovery. She clearly thought our entire family needed to drop everything to dance attendance on her.

Maman Diderot didn't like the idea of her daughter recuperating with only home health care and her maid to keep an eye on her, so she'd insisted Erica move into the dower house. That way, family could stop by and check in on her every day, and of course there was the help at the main house.

And that was why we were here in the old carriage house. Once it had been thoroughly cleaned and that musty smell gone, it was fine. Taylor moved into the main house because he needed his privacy, especially since he now had his first real boyfriend.

I liked having our privacy here, too. I wasn't fond of the Diderot House, never had been, and I really didn't like sleeping there overnight.

I was tired of not being in my own place. This was the longest I'd gone not living in my own place since the fire fifteen years ago. (It's a long story.)

I reached for the wool blanket we'd bought on a trip to Mexico and wrapped it around us both while Frank turned the television on, lowering the sound to not disturb Colin.

We'd all been lost when local weatherman and hurricane expert Nash Roberts had retired in the early aughts. The rule used to be to always watch Nash and do what he told you—if Nash said to go, you'd better pack up and hit the road. We'd finally settled on Lisette Reynolds as our new local trusted weatherperson. She was accurate most of the time, and let's face it, Nash wasn't Nash when he first started, either. Lisette, with her long auburn hair and gorgeous smile, was a local treasure.

I took another sip of coffee as another gust of wind slammed into the house. There was a loud bang outside, but I resisted the urge to get up and go look. None of the windows on the second floor had shutters, and there hadn't really been time to buy plywood and board them up. The windows had survived Katrina, so we felt pretty sure they'd be okay.

"Where's Scooter?" I asked. Scooter was our sweet orange cat that we originally got because there was a mouse somewhere in the house. Scooter might have the DNA of an apex jungle predator, but he was way too mellow to do anything like hunt. His favorite thing to do was sleep, and preferably in someone's lap. Taylor had grown really attached to him, but Scooter had come to the carriage house with us. He hadn't been in bed when I got up, and he wasn't anywhere around us, which was unusual. "Did you feed him?"

Frank looked away from Lisette, who was talking to someone in a raincoat and hood getting blasted by the wind and the rain on the lakeshore. He was standing on the lake wall, which wasn't something I'd be willing to do, especially since the water in the lake was rising. Hester was driving a storm surge in front of her, and that was always the big worry with hurricanes here—the storm surge. It was storm surge that did in the levees with Katrina, well, along with their faulty construction and maintenance. Lisette was even saying that very thing to him, and that he needed to get off the wall. His name flashed across the bottom of the screen again, and I smiled a bit. *Jason Childress.* Covered in plastic and other rain gear, his face wasn't clear to the camera because of rain getting the lens wet, but I knew what Jason Childress looked like.

He was kind of a snack, to be honest.

New Orleans has always been, and always will be, a very small town. Everyone knew everyone here—or was no more than two degrees of separation from everyone else. Jason had come to work for the local news station a little over a year ago, usually did weather on weekends or covered for Lisette when she was on vacation. He was pretty for a pale blond with what used to be called a peaches-and-cream complexion. He tanned to a nice golden shade, and his white-blond hair turned even whiter, but he always had apple-red cheeks, the kind adults love to pinch on children. He worked out at our gym, too—Riverview Fitness in Canal Place—and so I'd seen him naked in the locker room or drenched in sweat while doing his own workouts. I got strong gay vibes from him, despite the naturally deep and charming voice and the kind of pinup looks that drove teenage girls crazy and made them squeal. I hadn't heard anything about him but would probably run into him in one of the Quarter gay bars at some point. Probably Southern Decadence in a couple of weeks. All the city gays turned out for Southern Decadence.

Or he could be in a monogamous same-sex marriage and never went out.

Another blast of wind screamed around the building. I took another swig of my coffee. Lisette was now in front of the radar map. "The eye will pass over the Rigolets, based on the current projections from the Hurricane Center," she was saying. "In another few hours or so, give or take, but we are on the western side of the storm, so we'll be getting rain almost constantly until the final remnants have passed."

"Cell tower is down," Frank observed, frowning at the screen of his phone. "But the Wi-Fi is working."

"I hope we don't lose power," I said. Losing power here wasn't the end of the world; Diderot House had a generator with a natural gas line Papa Diderot had put in after Katrina. If we lost power, we'd just move over to the main house and sleep on the first floor until power was restored. Taylor had sneered at our privilege when I'd mentioned the generator when a storm was in the Gulf a few years ago, but I was betting he'd be grateful for said privilege if the power went out.

There was another loud crash from outside, like something had hit against one of the garage doors.

"We should probably see what that was," Frank said. "It sounded pretty big."

I stood up. "I'll go. You stay here and keep the couch warm." I reached down and kissed the top of his head. "Back in a jiffy."

I galloped down the stairs to the door leading into the garage. I opened it and flipped the light switch. The first floor always kind of gave me the creeps. There was a lot of furniture under white dustcloths that had yellowed with age, boxes and boxes in haphazard piles everywhere, and I thought, not for the first time, *this place really needs to be organized. I bet I could get Taylor to do it if I offered him the right amount of money*, before turning to face the big garage doors. There was another door right next to the big garage doors, the one that led to the street. There was a window in that door. I walked over to it and stood up on my tiptoes to see if I could get a look without opening the door.

No luck.

I looked around and found a big blue-and-white umbrella in an elephant's paw stand that would have sent Taylor into a tirade about big game hunting. I carried it back over to the door. Another gust blasted the house, shaking it a little bit, and I opened the umbrella.

In a fluid motion I opened the door and turned the umbrella to catch most of the wind and the rain but still had to back up a few steps. But finally, in a lull, I worked my way back to the doorframe, shoved the umbrella through the opening, and stepped into a puddle. The gutters were full of water, and water was starting to come up over the curb onto the cobblestone sidewalk.

There was a figure lying on the cement in front of the garage door, soaking wet.

It was almost obscured by the large live oak branch that had slammed into the building—I turned to look across the street and saw the scar where the wind had torn it off the tree on the other side.

Had the branch hit someone?

I stepped closer, and the wind snatched the umbrella, turning it inside out and ripping it out of my hands, sending it bouncing away down the cobblestones. I was drenched immediately. I tried to shield my eyes from the rain, which the wind was whipping into my body. The drops felt like needles trying to tear my skin open. My feet splashed through the puddles. As I reached down to check the form, lightning cracked and made everything bright as day outside as the thunder started rolling.

I stepped back in shock, recognizing the dead white face of Aunt Erica's daytime nurse, Kristin.

CHAPTER TWO

TWO OF SWORDS, REVERSED

Caution about dealing with the unscrupulous

My heart sank. Looking down at her sopping wet face, I closed my mind and thought: Here we go again.

Yes, I know. Callous and cold, right? But I've stumbled over so many dead bodies over the last fifteen years I think I can be forgiven for that initial reaction.

This was a new wrinkle, though. I'd never stumbled over a body hours before a hurricane hit the city.

Water running down my face, I leaned down and picked up her left hand, pressing my index finger to her wrist. Nothing. The skin was cold and soaked, though. There was something clutched in her left hand. I pried her fingers apart and slid the wet paper into the pocket of my sweatpants. I then put my fingertips to her carotid artery, pushing some leaves out of the way to get to her neck. Nothing. For the last chance, I put my hand just above her lips—blue beneath pink lipstick that hadn't washed off—and no air was coming out.

And there were bruises on her neck. Like she'd been strangled.

Another gust of wind almost knocked me over. I put my hands down on the wet concrete to balance better. I put my hand over my eyes to block as much of the downpour as possible so I could see, but a glance up Chestnut Street toward First showed no signs of life. No cars were parked along either side of the street, and no lights were on in the house on the other side of the street. The wind was bending the palm trees inside the stucco-covered brick wall along our property line. Another small branch came flying at me from the same live oak that donated its big branch to Nurse Kristin—what was her last name? Picot? Petit? Perrier? Something Cajun like that, anyway. I thought she was from up near Baton Rouge originally.

There was another flash of lightning nearby, followed by thunder that rolled for several moments. The wind picked up again, and I shivered.

I needed to get out of the storm.

As I was splashing back to the door, my synapses fired. Kristin was Erica's home care nurse. Who was with Aunt Erica?

I stepped out of the rain, shaking water off my head.

What was Kristin *doing* here?

I didn't know how long she'd been out there, but she'd felt cold to the touch.

Had Erica demanded she come to work the day of a hurricane?

Surely not even Aunt Erica was *that* demanding and awful.

Yeah, right. That's *exactly* the kind of person she was—spoiled, mean, and entitled. She loved nothing more than making a waitress weep. She was the original *I want to speak to a manager* white woman mold whence all the others sprang.

And Nurse Kristin—Picot?...that didn't seem right—was dead. She was already dead when the wind tore the branch off the tree. *Of course* it landed on her—this was New Orleans, and that's the kind of crazy thing that happens here all the time. But her body was too cold for this to have been recent. Her lips were already blue. Sure, it was cooler with the heavy rain, and the wind was making me shiver, but the weather was still too warm for her body to have gotten that cold quickly.

Her body had been lying there for quite a while.

During a hurricane? Who would be out on the night

before a hurricane arrived, dumping bodies? She could have been strangled here, on the street in front of the carriage house. The neighborhood had emptied out some—I'd noticed people loading up cars yesterday, not willing to wait and miss the already too-short evacuation window. The Garden District's private security had stopped patrolling last night because of the storm.

She could have been out there all night.

I didn't like the sound of that.

Frank came back down the stairs toward me, carrying my steaming mug and carrying a bath sheet. I closed the door just as the wind picked up again and goose bumps came up all over my body as I started shivering.

"Was there a body underneath that branch?" Frank asked, handing me the coffee and then wrapping the bath sheet around me, drying my head and neck while I clung to the hot cup and sipped.

"Uh-huh," I replied through chattering teeth. "It's Aunt Erica's nurse, Kristin." I took another gulp of hot coffee, feeling my shivering body starting to warm up. "Bruising on her neck, too, like she was strangled."

"Come on, let's get you upstairs and out of those wet clothes," Frank commanded, putting the chain on the door. I started following him up the stairs, and he said, over his shoulder, "So, Kristin Peltier? What on earth was she doing down here?"

Picot, Peltier, I'd been close.

I said, "Was she supposed to come to work today?"

"I don't think so," Frank said as he opened the door at the top of the stairs. "We all moved Erica up to the main house yesterday afternoon, while you were out getting supplies." I could hear the eye roll in his voice. Like Mom, Frank was also not a big fan of Aunt Erica's. "She complained about everything, of course, and made the whole process a lot harder than it needed to be. I thought Maman was going to stroke out at one point, but she just sighed and headed for the brandy. Erica was insisting that she had to have her nurse there during the day, but the night nurse called out as it was, so…"

I walked down the hallway into the big room. "No pulse, her lips are blue, and I saw bruising on her neck," I said, slipping out of my clothes and putting them in the sink. "I hate leaving her out there, but it's a crime scene. I shouldn't have messed with it as it was, but…"

"We need to call the police," Frank said.

"I hate to make them come out during a hurricane," I replied.

"We don't have a choice." Frank shrugged. "No telling what'll happen to the body—and no telling what evidence might have already washed away. And at least the full force of the storm isn't here yet. Maybe they can get the body sent off to the morgue before the worst of it hits." He shook his head. "Nothing worse than rain on a crime scene."

"Call Venus," I said, "while I take a shower and warm up." New Orleans rain was a force all on its own and didn't require a hurricane to make it misbehave. Every summer, the forecast for about six months was *hot, humid, chance of rain*. We've all gotten caught out in the rain so many times we could stock a secondhand umbrella shop. Whenever you're caught in the New Orleans rain, you always wind up trying your best to stay dry until the deluge defeats you and you give up, surrendering to getting a thorough soaking. I always needed to take a shower after getting soaked on the way home. I was always grouchy until I reset, and a shower did the trick.

Colin was still sleeping on his side, still slightly snoring as I dug through a drawer to find underwear, a sweatshirt, and sweatpants. As I got into the shower, my mind started clicking into gear as the hot water warmed my skin.

It looked like Kristin was wearing navy-blue scrubs, best as I could tell.

I hated calling Blaine and Venus out in this weather, but

the cops and other first responders were all on call and on duty.

Of all times for me to stumble over a body.

You never got used to it. It didn't freak me out as much as it did the first few times, but there's no better teacher than experience, right?

Why would someone want to kill a home care nurse?

I couldn't hazard a guess because I didn't know much about Kristin Peltier. I'd only seen her a few times, since she spent most of her time at the dower house. We'd bumped into each other in the kitchen at the main house a few times. She wasn't overly friendly, but she wasn't cold, either. She'd always been polite and professional, and I felt sorry for her. I'd feel sorry for anyone taking care of Aunt Erica.

Frank didn't think she was supposed to come to work today. She usually was on duty from eight in the morning until about five or six, and the night nurse came on duty later in the evening. I didn't know Kristin well because my distaste for Aunt Erica kept me from the dower house. When I was twelve years old, we'd been here for Christmas. I'd had more than enough family time so had gone out on the side gallery to just decompress from the unwanted questions from relatives, and I heard voices below. I recognized Aunt Erica's voice.

"You just mark my words," she was saying smugly, "Scotty'll come to a bad end, and it's good enough for her, always thinking she's so much better than me. All three of those kids are going to turn out as embarrassments to the entire family. I don't know how Mom and Dad can hold their heads up in polite society anymore."

I went back inside the house. I never said anything to anyone, especially not to Mom—she'd probably slug Erica, and Mom had a great right hook—but I also never forgot it, either.

I felt bad that she'd broken her hip, but not bad enough to help take care of her.

When her beloved stepson fled the country to avoid police charges, I thought about asking her how she thought Maman and Papa could hold their heads up in polite society after that disgrace, but why bother? She was the kind of person who thought she could say whatever she wanted to anyone, no matter how cruel or mean, but God forbid you returned the favor.

I dried off and got dressed. I felt a thousand times better than I had before the shower. I didn't hear rain or wind. Probably between storm bands.

"You're sure she wasn't supposed to come to work today?" I asked as I walked back into the big living area. "Did you call Venus?"

Frank clicked mute on the television, where Lisette Reynolds was gesticulating wildly as she used her Sharpie on a blue-screened satellite image of southeast Louisiana. "She and Blaine are on their way—she's calling out the Lab."

The Lab is what crime scene units were called here—the Louisiana State Police Crime Laboratory.

"Trust me," Frank continued, "I helped them move her up to the main house. I witnessed the entire argument."

"Nurse Peltier didn't want to come to work?"

"No, she wanted to come to work. Erica wanted her to come to work. Maman thought it was ridiculous, especially since we were moving her up to the main house." He scowled. "Your aunt is a textbook narcissist."

I'd never been close to Aunt Erica, even before I overheard her talking shit about me. I'd avoided her as much as possible ever since. She'd always seemed bitter and unlikable to me. She always said the most horrible things and then laughed, like it amused her to hurt people's feelings. She also liked to drink a lot. Nothing wrong with that, of course. Most people in New Orleans drank more than people in other cities, so those kinds of rules just didn't apply here. New Orleans probably had more functioning alcoholics than any other city in the world.

But the more she drank, the meaner she became. I know she tried Mom's patience a lot, and Mom had spent a lot of my life not on speaking terms with her sister, to my relief.

It made sense. You never thought about your family member being mentally ill or having a personality disorder. We'd always written it off as her being jealous of my mother, or any number of other scarring things that happen to everyone in this family on a regular basis.

I came by my unconventionality genetically.

But narcissism? Now that he'd said it, I absolutely saw it. Everything had to be about Aunt Erica, and if it wasn't, she would do her best to make it about her. Rain said Erica had a bad case of main character syndrome when she was, at best, a walk-on cameo. She was exhausting to deal with.

"You poor thing," I said. I wasn't sorry they'd moved her while I was out getting supplies. It had taken forever, traffic had been obnoxious, and the shelves had already been picked over. No water, toilet paper, or paper towels. Fortunately, my grandparents had a fully stocked liquor cabinet, because there was nothing left except the toxic stuff that eats paint.

I would never be that desperate.

I sat down on the couch next to Frank and slipped my arm around him. "Sorry you had to deal with that. I think you're right—she's a narcissist, all right. That would explain so much."

"It sounds like the storm is letting up a bit," he said. "We must be between bands. This is a good chance for me to run over to the main house—"

"Just call." I hooked my leg over his. "You don't want to get caught."

Frank gave me a look. "Don't you think it's better if I go over there and tell them in person that there's a dead body outside?" He shook his head. "They'll have a million questions, and—"

"They'll worry if we're safe or not," I finished for him.

We did tend to wind up in dangerous situations more often than most. A phone call would just make everyone over there more nervous, or one of them would come to check. "You wait for Venus, I'll go over there."

"Scotty—" He started to argue but stopped when I kissed him.

I galloped down the back stairs to check on the crime scene situation.

I opened the front door and got a blast of water in my face. Water was cascading like a waterfall from the awning over the door. The wind grabbed the door out of my hands and slammed it against the stucco wall. Water was running down the slope of the yard. All the yard furniture had been taken into the carriage house yesterday. We'd drained the pool as a precaution because the chlorinated water would damage the lawn, and my grandfather spent too much money on the yard to take a chance on chlorine burns. I hurried as fast as I could over the soft, wet ground, my feet sinking into mud more than I would have liked. The wind was coming from behind me, so that helped propel me forward, but I was also shivering, and the rain… Water was pouring off me as I went up the brick back steps to the back gallery. Once I was on the back gallery, the overhanging roof blocked the rain. I shook rain off me, squeezed out my sweatpants, and before I could even turn around, the back door was open a crack.

It was Nora, my grandparents' current housekeeper.

"Scotty, what are you doing out there? Have you lost your mind?" She opened the door wide, grabbed me by the arm, and started dragging me inside with surprising strength. Nora was in her late fifties and wore her thick steel-gray and white hair in a braid she coiled around her head. Her glasses were tortoiseshell and simple.

Helga, who'd worked for my grandparents for most of my life, wore a uniform every day, long after Maman told her she didn't have to. Nora wasn't yet considered a member of the family, and I didn't know much about her. I just knew she was a widow, she'd retired from a teaching job, and her children were all grown and on their own. I thought being a housekeeper was an odd second-career choice, but Maman said Nora loved housekeeping. Papa and Maman hadn't thought they would be able to find someone who could live in, which was their preference. Nora had been working as the housekeeper at one of the plantation houses along the River Road, closer to Baton Rouge, and was happy to sell her house and move down to the city. She was even more efficient than Helga had been, and Maman became a starry-eyed fan when she'd managed to save twenty percent on average on groceries.

I wasn't sure what to make of Nora, to be honest. My grandparents worshipped her, but she seemed guarded and distant to me. Or maybe she was just different from Helga. Different didn't mean worse.

"Let me get you a towel. Stay there and don't drip on my floor. It was waxed yesterday." She slipped through a door that led to the laundry room while I obediently stayed in place just inside the door. I looked back out through its window, but I couldn't see the dower house through the gloom and the rain.

Nora returned after a few moments carrying a bundle, which she started handing to me piecemeal. First a towel, which I quickly ran over my body, then some shapeless sweatpants and an enormous fluffy robe so white it was almost blinding. I dried my feet before slipping them into the too-big slippers and tied the robe closed. Then I slipped out of my sweatpants and underwear. She held out her hands for my wet clothes, which I handed to her.

"I'll put these in the dryer," she said, adding, "and when I get back, I expect a logical explanation for what you're doing out in a hurricane."

"It's between bands," I called after her, pouring myself a cup of coffee. "Well, that's the thing. Frank said y'all moved Aunt Erica up here from the dower house yesterday."

"Well, it just made sense, you know, your aunt not really being able to fend for herself just yet." She nodded. "Last night we still thought it might not be a hurricane and told Kristin it was better and made more sense for her to either stay the night here, or just go home and not worry about coming in today, we'd manage without her. Just more work for me, but I don't mind." She shook her head. "The night nurse, Bracken, had to go up to the Northshore to keep an eye on his parents and get them out, if need be, so we thought it was just better to move her up here." She shook her head. "She doesn't need to be waited on hand and foot, either. She needs to get up with her walker and move around or she's always going to be an invalid." Her eyes opened wide. "Oh, my apologies, Mr. Scott, I—"

"How many times have I told you just call me Scotty?" I took a sip from the cup. It was hot, fresh, and so strong I could feel my chest hair growing. The robe was soft, warm, and comfortable.

"And how many times do I have to tell you I'm not getting into that habit?" Her brown eyes twinkled behind her practical eyeglasses. "Then one day I'll call your grandfather *Lucien*, and he'll send me packing with his curses ringing in my ears."

I considered arguing that Papa Diderot would never fire her for so minor an infraction as familiarity but dropped it. She was different from Helga, who'd been with the family so long she talked back to Papa Diderot without a hint of fear. "Okay, but call me Mr. Scotty, at least."

"Mr. Scotty." She smiled, but it didn't reach her eyes. "Yes, I can do that." Her brow wrinkled. "What does your aunt moving up here to the main house have to do with you being out in the storm?"

"So, Kristin—what was her last name?"

"Pitre." Ha! Frank had also been wrong.

"So was Kristin Pitre coming to work today or not?"

"She insisted that she'd come, and if she had to, she'd come even earlier since Bracken couldn't make it." She nodded. "I told her to call if she was coming, but she never did. When I saw Hester had been upgraded to a hurricane, I figured that was why." She glanced over at the clock. "It's almost eight, and she hasn't called, so I guess she isn't coming." She snorted. "You wouldn't have to tell me twice not to come to work on a hurricane day. Who wants to come to work the day of a hurricane if they don't have to?"

"Maybe she did try to make it," I replied. "She's on the sidewalk outside the carriage house. The wind blew a big branch from that live oak across the street into the back side of the carriage house. When I went out to see what it was, I found her lying there, under the branch and in front of one of the garage doors. Frank called the police, but I thought I'd come up here and find out—"

"Dead?" Nora gasped, taking a step back. "Did the branch kill her?"

"All I know for sure is she's dead," I replied, not wanting to share the murder news. I'd let Venus and Blaine do that part. "She could have had a heart attack for all I know. But she knew that Aunt Erica had been moved up here at the main house?"

Nora nodded, looking unwell. "She supervised it. It was her idea, and your grandparents thought it a good one."

I scratched my chin. "You're sure she didn't call?"

"I'm sure." Nora fished a phone out of her pocket. She pulled up the call log and held it out to me. "No calls since yesterday afternoon. It's weird that she drove in from Kenner without calling." She frowned. "Maybe she called your aunt instead. She is in the library—I'd just taken her breakfast when I saw you out there on the gallery. Ask her."

"Thanks." I drained the coffee cup and headed out of the kitchen down the hall to the big library.

The library was always my favorite room in my grandparents' house. It was more of a study, really, the room where the gentlemen would retire after dinner for brandy and cigars and relax, back in the olden days. Sexist bullshit, of course, it was very much a man's world back then. That was why Mom always called it the library rather than the study and why I did, too. It was a gorgeous room and was often featured in design magazines because the room's design elements were virtually unchanged from how they had looked originally. Dark mahogany paneling covered the walls, where they weren't broken up by built-in bookshelves or the fireplace. I loved the bay window, which held a big seat with pillows and blankets for comfortable sitting and reading. The windows were latticed in a slanted pattern, which always broke up the light streaming in into interesting shapes on the huge antique Oriental rug. There used to be a desk in here when Papa Diderot used it as a working office. But he'd retired from doing any kind of work years ago, so the desk had been taken out and replaced with a lovely low coffee table, carved out of a solid block of oak and stained beautifully. Every little table was adorned with an antique Tiffany lamp. There was an enormous Audubon print over the fireplace that was worth more than I wanted to think about.

Aunt Erica's hospital bed had been set up in the center of the room, placed so direct sunlight from any of the windows would never touch a corner of the bed. She was awake and reading *The Drowning Tree* by Carol Goodman. A metal carafe of coffee was on the small table next to the bed, next to a heavy, amber-colored glass ashtray overflowing with ash and lipstick-stained Benson & Hedges butts. She didn't look up at first as I stood on the room's threshold and watched her.

Aunt Erica had been pretty when she was a young woman. I'd seen enough pictures of those days—there certainly were enough of them decorating the walls of this place—but there was no trace of the beautiful wistful young woman depicted in those photographs in the face I was looking at. Her hair was completely white, thinning, and pulled back so severely from her face it looked painful. She had always been small and was diminishing more as she aged. Her face was weathered and lined, and her false teeth were so perfect they looked real. She was wearing a light blue nightgown with a high neck, and her lower body was covered in blankets. A walker and a wheelchair had been discreetly tucked away into corners of the room.

She looked up from her book and scowled at me. "Just going to hover in the damned doorway or are you coming in?" she asked. Her voice was similar to Mom's, but there was this underlying whiny tone in her voice that always grated on me.

Kind of like the way it was doing right now.

I forced a smile on my face and tried to remember to be kind. So what if she was a narcissist? (Frank's diagnosis, confirming Mom's, was good enough for me; as a retired Fed, he had a lot of experience with personality disorders.) She'd had a rough life. Her third husband's children, whom she'd claimed as her own despite not raising them, had been a handful. The middle child had fled to Europe to escape prosecution for assaulting an ex the summer of Katrina. I didn't remember the details that much. I'd never really known her stepson and hadn't liked what I did know. She'd been his biggest cheerleader, though. That much I remembered from fourteen years ago.

I cleared my throat. "Aunt Erica, have you heard from your day nurse Kristin today?"

She rolled her eyes. "Have you not noticed we're in the middle of a tropical storm?" she said, her words dripping with sarcasm.

Instead of rising to her bait, I did what Mom always recommended—fight her with sugar. I forced a smile on my face. "I was curious since I found her dead body outside the carriage house today." I kept my voice polite and even, like it wasn't a big deal.

I wondered how long it would take for her to make Kristin's death about her.

Her face blanched, her mouth opening and closing a few times as she reached for her phone. She held it up to her face, tapped at the screen with her fingers, and finally said, in a choked voice, "No, nothing. I insisted she stay home and not risk her life coming in to take care of me!" Her voice quivered. "And now you're telling me that she was coming in, despite the danger, and lost her life? Because of *me*? How awful." Her eyes began to get watery, and her voice was getting a self-pitying whine to it. The big dramatic meltdown was on its way. "How…how did it happen?"

Less than a minute, I thought, before saying out loud, my tone gentler, "Something big hit the carriage house, and I went out to see what it was and if there was any damage. That's when I found her." Aunt Erica had always treated servants like something she'd stepped in, and I was certain she'd put Kristin in that category. I've never understood being nasty to people who help you. I hoped she'd been paying Kristin what she was worth.

Because there wasn't enough money in the world for me to put up with her.

Probably a good thing I hadn't gone into nursing.

"I'm not sure what happened," I went on. "I just wanted to check in with you, see what you knew, if anything." Interesting. Nora had said Kristin was planning on coming in. I patted Erica's hand gently and wasn't surprised when she jerked it away. "It was probably an accident or something, but Frank was calling the cops, and I volunteered to come talk to everyone up here, see what was up and warn you so you wouldn't panic when you see the police lights."

Kristin must have planned to come to work this morning and just hadn't called Nora. She'd driven in from Kenner during a tropical storm, not wanting the responsibility of her patient's care in the hands of the family.

Erica's face screwed up into a sneer, but then it suddenly relaxed, went softer. Her eyes filled again. "Oh. Maman!" she cried, holding out her arms. "Have you heard about poor Kristin? Scotty was just telling me about it! It's just so awful!" She buried her face in her hands and started sobbing. It seemed like an act to me, but I wasn't her mother.

Mom always said Erica was different when their parents were around. I'd noticed it myself more than once.

And here we went again.

Maman bit her lip. She was wearing her black silk robe and had a scarf tied around her head. "Is this true?"

I nodded, giving her a hug. "I better get back to talk to the police when they get here."

Maman nodded, hugged me back, and held out her arms as she walked to her sobbing daughter's bedside.

I left them to each other and slipped back out of the room, shutting the door behind me as I heard Erica sob, "He didn't even ask me how I was doing!"

I rolled my eyes and walked back to the kitchen.

CHAPTER THREE
THE HANGED MAN
A period of indecision

There was no sign of Nora when I walked back into the kitchen. My ratty old sweats were neatly folded on the island in the center of the big kitchen, my underwear on the very top. I walked back over to the back door. I wiped away some of the condensation on the glass and saw it was just sprinkling. I might be able to make it back to the carriage house before the next band gets here, I thought. I changed back into my own clothes, tossing the baggy, borrowed ones into the laundry hamper. On second thought, I grabbed the robe to wear for the dash back to the carriage house. The hood was big enough to drape down over my head, so I could keep rain from getting into my eyes.

It would work while it was just sprinkling.

I walked back through the kitchen and opened the back door.

The damp warm air smacked me across the face. The back gallery was slick with water, and my flip-flops were so worn out there was hardly any grip left to the soles. I took them off and slid them into the pocket of the robe. The last thing I needed to do was take a fall—barefoot was probably safer. The water had mostly drained out of the yard while I was inside, but the wet grass would be slippery.

With the flagstone path no longer underwater, I made my way over to it carefully, slipping on the wet grass or when my foot came down in soupy mud. I stepped onto the marble flagstones. *That wasn't so bad now, was it?* The carriage house didn't look *that* far away, but the grounds were huge for being in the city.

When I was a kid, my grandparents' house and grounds had been like a magic kingdom to me. The Diderots have always been proud of how big the lot was, and over a hundred and fifty years of work on the grounds had made it look like a park. The grass was usually thick and soft and a rich verdant green. With the banana ferns and palm trees and fountains and live oaks, my grandparents' property had been a playground. Flowerbeds nestled every kind of bloom imaginable. The grounds always kind of hummed with insects—flies and bees and butterflies—and we were always slapping at mosquitoes, gnats, and fleas. By contrast, the big house with its dark wooden paneling and valuable antiques intimidated me when I was a kid. I always felt uncomfortable in that house and tried to never spend the night there. I always had nightmares when I did.

It always felt like someone—or something—was there, just out of sight. Sometimes I might see something out of the corner of my eye.

And it's not like there weren't about a million legends and ghost stories about the house.

I picked my way over the flagstones carefully. A strong chilly gust of wind blasted me, flipping the hood back off my head, and I took my eyes off where I was stepping. I put a foot down and half missed the next slippery stone. I lost my balance immediately and remembered to not try to catch myself and to go limp.

I landed on the wet grass hard, knocking all the air out of my lungs at once. Little lights danced and spun in my eyes as I stared up, wheezing and gasping for air, at the black and gray clouds overhead. As if on cue, a big fat raindrop hit *splat* in my right eye. Wincing—my back was aching and so was my ankle—I sat up, grateful the yard had drained from the last downpour. I took a few deep breaths and checked everything. Ribs felt fine, lower back fine, arms and legs okay—just some throbbing that would probably go away with the help of some acetaminophen. As I watched, the clouds started moving a lot faster than they had when I'd come outside. That meant the next band was coming in soon.

I had to get moving.

At least no one saw it happen, I reminded myself. Colin and Frank would have howled with laughter while making sure I was okay, of course, and I'd have had to listen to their jokes for weeks.

The thick fluffy robe, so warm and comforting when I'd put it on, was now soaked in the back. It felt like it weighed a gazillion pounds. I shrugged it off and started trying to wring some of the water out as I started walking more carefully this time. The back of the robe was filthy, too. I didn't want to think about how dirty the bottoms of my feet must be.

And once I was inside, I was going to stay inside until the storm passed. No more going outside.

I couldn't see why I'd have to, but then, we already had a dead body, and the storm wasn't even here yet.

And if life has taught me anything, it's that things tend to be out of control once a dead body shows up.

It started sprinkling again as I picked my way over the flagstones, avoiding slick-looking spots. I was starting to get a headache—either sinus pressure from the storm or I hit my head, which I didn't remember doing, but who knew? The air was feeling a lot thicker and heavier by the time I got to the little wooden awning over the front door to the carriage house. I reached for the handle and froze as I remembered I hadn't taken my keys. It used to be a running joke in the early days with the boys—I'd always forget something when leaving the house, keys or wallet or sometimes both. The teasing worked. I stopped forgetting things. I was better organized than I used to be, but Frank still despaired.

But the knob turned, because of course Frank figured I didn't take my keys. I tried to close the door behind me, but a gust of wind came around the corner of the building and ripped it out of my hands. It slammed into the wall with a loud bang. I grabbed and slammed it shut behind me, flipping the deadbolt closed, just in case. The wind had blown some sheets off old furniture and disturbed a lot of dust. I coughed and shivered as I started up the stairs to the apartment.

I was almost to the back door to the apartment when everything went white and every hair on my body stood up. The thunder that followed immediately was deafening, and the sky opened like a spigot being turned on. I could hear the television. I walked in and dropped my robe into the laundry basket. The rain pattered on the roof, and another gust of wind buffeted the building. I wearily trudged to the coffee maker. Colin was awake now and sitting on the couch, absorbed in his laptop. Frank put down his phone and frowned at me.

"What happened to you?" he asked.

"I fell on the way back, but no big deal," I replied.

"We're just waiting for the cops," Frank said. "From the sound of things, it may be a while." He looked up at the ceiling. The rain was coming down so hard it sounded like the drops might pierce the roof.

Not looking up, Colin smiled. "Leave it to Scotty to find a body right before a hurricane gets here."

"If it wasn't him, it would have been me." Frank flushed a bit. "I would have gone down to check to see what it was if he hadn't."

I did a double take. Frank was passing up a chance to double-team me? Must be the hurricane weather. It did make people act weird.

"And found Kristin Pitre," I said, making another cup of

coffee as my teeth started to chatter. "Her name is—*was*—Kristin Pitre. Nora said Kristin originally insisted on coming in this morning, but the way they left things, she was supposed to call this morning about whether she'd make it in or not—"

"The way New Orleans people think they can do things and function normally during tropical weather will never cease to amaze me." Colin interrupted me with a wink. "I couldn't believe it when Frank said you'd walked over to the main house." He shook his head. "I thought when the hatches were battened, we were supposed to stay buckled down?"

"Well, it wasn't the smartest thing I've done—"

"Which is saying something," Frank interrupted with a smirk.

Okay, now things were back to normal since they were ganging up on me again. They both can be so annoying when they want to be. I have the patience of Job.

For some reason, people have always teased me. Storm and Rain and Mom and Dad were relentless, and even my friends loved to fuck with me. Sometime I'd have to unpack with my therapist why I was drawn to people who liked to annoy me, but that time wasn't right now.

"But I didn't want to just call over there and drop a bomb on everyone," I said in my snarkiest tone, raising an eyebrow and curling my lip. "And I wanted to talk to Aunt Erica and Nora to see what she was doing here this morning. Nora said she'd told Kristin not to think about it, they'd manage without her, but she kept insisting." I frowned. "It doesn't make sense to me she'd want to risk driving in."

"Well, she is a nurse…" Colin's voice trailed off. He made a face. "But it wasn't like Erica needed her, was it?"

"Nora said they'd left it that Kristin would call if she was coming in, so Nora could watch for her," I went on. "And I think it's very strange that she *planned* to come to work. But Nora said she'd never called, so she'd assumed she wasn't. She was just as surprised as we were."

"Thanks for talking to Erica so we don't have to." Frank winked at Colin. "So, are we going to try to solve this? During a hurricane?" He laughed. "That's a new one for us, anyway."

Were we too blasé about hurricanes and tropical weather in New Orleans? I could see why it looked like that to outsiders. But when you lived in harm's way every year from June to December, you also learned to live with it. You learned when you needed to go and when you could stay. What to take with you when you go and what could be left behind. You knew what kind of supplies to stock for a few days without power. But we tended to stay calm, and the more time passed between major storms, you tended to get complacent. It had been years since New Orleans was walloped the way Katrina did. When you lived in harm's way, you learned to always be alert and keep watch, but you could never get jaded. *Oh, I don't feel like getting supplies this time and it'll turn anyway* became *Oh it'll turn before it comes ashore, so I don't need to evacuate*, and then you had a storm like Hurricane Katrina for the first time in forty years, and you became hypervigilant.

I never used to evacuate.

I will always regret not leaving for Katrina.

All my life I'd heard people say things like *I don't evacuate for anything less than a Category 3*. Offices which usually closed when a storm was heading this way started requiring employees to come to work or use sick or vacation time if they evacuated. I mean, I got it. False alarms built up a false sense of security. Especially since whenever New Orleans was in harm's way, the national media and The Weather Channel got hard-ons and didn't bother hiding their excitement at the possibility of a horrible outcome.

That's why I liked Lisette Reynolds. She's not one of those, and she does get excited, but it's not unseemly. Probably because she lives in Lakeview.

"Well, I think hurricane overrules anything else—we can

leave this one to Venus and Blaine," I said with a lofty smile. But when his face fell, I added, "You can do some research online about Kristin, if you want to. I'm going to change out of these wet clothes." I grabbed more coffee before heading back to the bedroom.

This isn't our case. But it won't hurt to know more about Kristin, will it? I'm sure Maman did a thorough background check before hiring her, right? I thought as I hung my wet clothes over the shower rail to dry.

But I couldn't stop thinking about poor Kristin Pitre, lying dead out there in the rain. Since she stuck mostly to the dower house catering to Erica's every whim, I hadn't encountered her very often since we'd moved into the carriage house. Sometimes I'd see her in the main house's kitchen, and we'd exchange pleasantries. She was nice, polite and friendly, but didn't like answering any personal questions I asked to try to get to know her better. She lived in Kenner, she was originally from a small town in Livingston Parish, close to Baton Rouge, and she was single. Her parents were dead, and she didn't have much family—or so she said. She was never rude, always polite, just not interested in talking about herself. She would always turn the conversation back around to you. It was an excellent deflection tool, because who doesn't want to talk about themselves?

She also had to have the patience of a saint to deal with Aunt Erica. For all I knew, though, she considered Erica a dream patient. I turned on the hot water in the sink and washed my face and then used a washcloth to wash mud off my calves and feet. (I was so right about the bottoms of my feet.)

Why would anyone kill Nurse Pitre? How long had she been lying out there? How long would it have been before someone noticed her body lying outside had that branch not hit the garage door? I doubted any cops were out just patrolling neighborhoods. It's very hard to see in the pouring rain, especially at night, and even now visibility wasn't that great.

She'd been murdered, no question. Those ugly purple bruises on her neck weren't from a skin condition. Someone had strangled her, which meant they had to be strong, right? Because wouldn't she have struggled? Venus had once told me that stranglers tended to be very close to the victim—spouse, parent, child—because you had to get close to strangle them. Why would a stranger strangle someone when there were so many easier ways to kill someone? "It's usually a crime of passion, especially if they use their hands," she'd added.

Which made sense in a stomach-turning way. You really had to hate someone to choke them to death with your bare hands, and who hated someone more than someone who used to love them?

I wondered what time she'd been killed.

We had all been asleep. What time had Frank gotten up?

I pulled on a fresh pair of sweats and ran the towel over my head again. Feeling better, I wandered back out to the main room where they were both staring at their laptop screens on opposite sides of the dining table. Colin was closer, so I kissed the back of his neck before going around the table to do the same to Frank. I felt better, more awake. The caffeine was working. "Any updates on the storm?"

"You're not going to believe this." Frank sighed. "But it wobbled again and went back out to sea."

"*What?*" I gaped at him.

Colin nodded. "Yeah, afraid so, just like Isaac in—what year was that? 2012?"

"Yeah." I stifled a moan as I walked back to the coffee maker.

After Katrina, it was easy to count evacuations/direct hits because they seemed to always occur during the Republican National Convention for the most part. We hadn't evacuated for Isaac because, like Hester, it had only been a tropical storm/Category 1 when it came ashore. Isaac had come ashore south of the city and then gone back out into the Gulf before making landfall again and hitting New Orleans. It knocked out power for most of the city, but despite it being late August/early September, Isaac had dragged clouds and cooler weather behind him, and not having power was bearable. We hadn't even broken down and relocated to the Diderot House with its generator until the third day without power. We got power back the Friday night after Isaac's landfall shenanigans on Sunday and Monday.

"So, this hasn't even started." I sat back down at the table and moaned. "Well, maybe we won't lose power—"

"We'll survive," Colin cut me off. He cocked his head to one side. "Has it stopped raining? Maybe we should take another look at the body, while we have a chance." He whistled. "And the storm going back into the Gulf is just going to delay the cops getting here, no matter what Venus said."

"What time did you get up this morning, Frank?" I asked as I hunted for another pair of flip-flops. "You didn't hear anything?"

"Thunder woke me about six," he replied, standing and unfurling to his full height. He was naked beneath his baggy gray sweatpants and wasn't wearing a shirt. Fifteen years we'd been together, and his body still took my breath away. Since he stopped wrestling, he'd let his chest hair grow in. It's not like he's a bear or anything. There was a light dusting of dark hair over his torso, with the thickest patch the white one between his pecs. There was also a black treasure trail leading from his navel to his waistband. He'd always shaved it after he retired from the FBI and moved here, where he could finally be openly gay for the first time in his life—but gay aesthetics be damned, he looked sexy with chest hair.

He'd look sexy in a grocery bag.

Colin was shorter than both of us, barely managing five

foot seven on a good day—giving me an inch or two advantage, heightwise. But Colin weighed more than I did. He was built like a little muscled fireplug and had only put on more muscle since I'd first danced with him on the bar at the Pub all those years ago. He was olive-skinned, with bluish-black hair that came in curly when he let it grow out. Before he'd retired as an agent-for-hire, he'd always kept it cropped short because the curls stood out too much. His body was thick (*thicc*, as Taylor would say), but like Frank, he carried very little body fat, and the little pudge he was starting to develop around his waistline didn't detract from his spectacular looks at all. He had deep sparkling blue eyes (he also wore contacts a lot when in disguise) and deep dimples, and the thick muscle looked almost like steel slabs on his body. His hair was also growing in now, and I loved the little bluish-black curls forming on his scalp. He didn't have much chest hair, but his patches—around the nipples, in the center of his chest, a treasure trail—accentuated his muscles a lot more than shaving it smooth did. All he was wearing was a pair of gray workout shorts whose elastic waistband was losing its battle against gravity and time.

He also gave the best hugs.

"Y'all guys find out anything about Kristin online?" I asked as we started down the back steps.

"Not much," Frank replied. "She's in her early forties, originally born in Livingston Parish—Enid, I think was the town—and she got her nursing degree from LSU. She's never married, and her social media is private, friends-only. Parents deceased, and she has a sister who lives in Baton Rouge. Do you think we should call her?"

I already knew some of this from just talking to her. Frank sounded worried. He has a very rigid need to always do the right thing, instilled in him by an abusive and homophobic church, and his years with the FBI only made it worse. I loved that about him, but it got on my nerves at times. It took him months to get used to not being a Fed and relaxing around illicit drug use. Frank really had needed to move to New Orleans to get that stick out of his ass. "I mean, what if she's waiting to hear from her or is worried?"

"She lives in Kenner," Colin said from behind us, "and the power's out in Jefferson Parish on the east bank, I checked the Entergy map. And the last report wasn't sure when Hester would turn back—if she does, that is."

Hurricane tracking had never been an exact science.

"So, if the sister is worried, she'd check that map and see that she doesn't have power," Frank finished for him. "But I still think we should let her know."

"Better to come from the police, especially since we don't have any answers for her," I said, reaching up to unbolt the door and take the chain off. "I mean, they won't either, but at least they're official, not some strangers she doesn't know from Adam."

I pulled the door open to a still Garden District. The rain had stopped. Everything was dripping, but nothing moved. There was no wind. The sky was still gray, covered in clouds. There was maybe an inch of fast-moving water on the street, and the gutters were full.

I walked over to where Kristin's body was, Frank and Colin right behind me.

I pulled the branches back away from her face. Without the blinding rain, I could make out a lot more. Not only were there those nasty bruises on her neck, there was also a bruise on her right forehead, like she'd been struck. Whatever makeup she'd been wearing had been washed away by the heavy rain. Her lips were still blue, and her skin was the bluish-white of a fish belly. There was no expression on her face, so she hadn't been afraid or in pain when she'd died. She was wearing navy-blue scrubs, soaked through, and a clear plastic rain jacket over them. She didn't have her purse. I scanned the area looking for her car keys or her purse, and didn't see either.

Come to think of it, where was her car?

"What kind of car did she drive?" I asked. The pockets of the clear raincoat were empty, as were the pockets of the scrubs.

"She drove a blue Kia," Colin said, kneeling beside the body and placing two fingers where her carotid artery should be. "And she usually parked down by the dower house."

The driveway, a late addition years after the house was originally built in the mideighteenth century, formed a semicircle, and both ends were gated. The drive also branched off around the main house to the parking area in back by the dower house. The carriage house used to have a sidewalk leading to the house, but my grandparents had it broken up and removed as a hazard. Like all sidewalks in the city, it had buckled and broken into pieces, shredded by live oak roots and ground subsidence. They'd replaced it with the flagstones, which got mossy and slippery in this climate.

"So how did she end up outside the carriage house?" I asked, standing back up and letting Colin carefully—not touching or moving anything—examine the body. "If she drove, where's her car?"

Frank walked down to the corner at First Street and looked both ways. He held up both hands, shaking his head to indicate no sign of her car.

Okay, I thought. No sign of her keys or her purse or her car, which meant one of two things. Whoever had killed her could have stolen her purse and car, or she'd been killed here, her purse taken—but the car? Oh, and she could have been dumped here.

But why? Why would anyone kill a home care nurse from Kenner?

Oh, Scotty, you know as well as anyone that looks can be deceiving. There's no telling what she could have been up to in her private life. She could be at the center of a torrid love triangle or something.

I sat back on my haunches, resting my knees on the wet concrete.

Sure, that was possible, but I couldn't picture it.

The killer didn't care when the body was found, so he was confident he wouldn't get caught.

Why would the killer dump her body here?

Either way, doing so would bring my grandparents into it, and it was believable someone would be out to get Papa Diderot. Killing someone employed here certainly would cast a cloud of suspicion over the family, but we'd weathered worse storms than this before. Maybe it was misdirection, intended to get the cops to focus on the Diderots instead of on Kristin herself.

Everyone would look at the Diderots. It was genius, if diabolical.

Papa Diderot was a decent man with a few blind spots, if a bit cranky and opinionated. He'd lived quite a life in his ninety-plus years. He and Maman were the same age, looked thirty years younger, and were in perfect health. I'd always thought he was homophobic when I was younger but had found out after a family secret had come out (oh, yes, there were *lots* of those) that what I'd taken as homophobia was more concern about my safety living in a homophobic world. He was worried about me.

Sweet, but given how many dead bodies I'd stumbled over in the course of my adult life, his fears were clearly misplaced.

But he was also a wealthy businessman and scion of an old aristocratic Creole family in New Orleans. The first Diderot set foot in Louisiana territory in 1724, only six years after the town was founded. The closets of Diderot House were filled with skeletons going back several centuries. I'd heard some of the stories, which are mostly legends that have been embellished in an ongoing game of generational telephone within the family. Maman's family, the Miltons, were descended from a ne'er-do-well British grifter who'd come to town during King George's War and made his money in land speculation before settling upriver on the German Coast—and there were lots of secrets and skeletons in their closets, too.

I know the Diderot Trust, which controlled my money, had some questionable investments. I'd requested, once I'd seen my portfolio, that going forward *my* trust wasn't investing in evil corporations, and to divest any investments in any companies that were red flags to me. Well, most companies were evil—what else was profits before people, but a social evil?—but I wanted my investments to be in renewables and companies that did some good in the world.

I tried not to think about the parts of our family history where my ancestors enslaved people. It's hard to respect ancestors that were human traffickers.

We couldn't rule out Kristin's murder had something to do with the family.

But where to start?

You don't, you leave it to the police.

I pulled out my phone and started photographing Kristin Pitre's body. There could be other wounds we couldn't see, hidden beneath the branch. The rains would have washed away any blood from wounds down into the storm sewers.

There was yet another flash of lightning so close it was just white light. There wasn't even a second to process the burning smell of ozone when thunder clapped so loudly that my ears rang. It literally sounded like the sky had cracked open. It started sprinkling again, and the wind started picking up just as a police patrol car came sliding around the corner at Philip Street at the other end of the block. Their blue lights were on, but no sirens. Smart, I thought, no need to make anyone else in the neighborhood nervous.

I stood up and waved at them as a strong gust of wind almost blew me over. The light sprinkle started coming down harder, with bigger drops that stung on contact. The police car rolled up past me, stopping alongside the gutter. I stood motionless, keeping my hands visible.

You could never be sure with a cop, and why tempt fate?

Both doors opened on either side, and two Black cops emerged, wearing clear plastic raincoats over their uniforms. "Y'all call in a dead body?" the driver called over to me. He was taller than his partner, and bigger.

"Yes," I replied, pointing down. "I'm Scotty Bradley, my grandparents own the house"—I gestured toward the main house—"and her name is Kristin Pitre. She worked for my aunt as a home care nurse."

"And she was coming in today?" the second cop asked, his voice incredulous. It was higher pitched than his partner's, but he gave the impression of coiled strength.

"That's the thing—she was supposed to call the housekeeper and let her know if she was coming, but she never did." I made a face. "When the branch hit the garage door, we came down to see what it was, and that was, um, when we found her." I didn't mention anything about her car. Better to let them come to their own conclusions—and beat cops generally didn't like helpful civilians. It had taken Blaine and Venus years to get to the point where we didn't drive them crazy. I thought they were fonder of us than they used to be, but that just might be me.

"Y'all might as well get inside and stay dry," he replied. "Crime Lab will be here soon, and Detectives Tujague and Casanova will be here as soon as possible. Where will you be when they need to talk to you?"

I pointed back to the open door. "Just have them ring the bell."

And I thought our work there was done.

You'd think I'd know better by now.

Chapter Four

The Hermit

Silent counsel

Colin went upstairs to get the officers coffee. I lingered at the door for a moment. That band had passed, and the rain had stopped other than a light, almost unnoticeable sprinkle. The gusty wind had also slowed. I watched the two uniforms cordon off the crime scene with orange cones and two bright red flares they put in the street. I shivered.

The calm between storm bands was eerie. After the howling and rattling of the wind and the downpour, the quiet was unsettling. It felt like the storm was resting, revving up to try to rip us off the ground once again. The cloudy sky just kind of glowed gray, and everything was so still. The inch of water on the street was draining into the gutters. Water also gushed out from around the brick fence on the property's First Street side. On this side street, the fence was brick under stucco with a big iron gate alongside the carriage house. Water was also squeezing out underneath that gate and was probably deeply pooled on the other side. Like most brick fences in New Orleans, ours no longer stood at a ninety-degree angle to the ground, leaning toward the sidewalk at a dangerous-looking, collapse-is-imminent angle. Some of the painted stucco had broken away in places, exposing the brick beneath, and hadn't been repaired. The side street side of the carriage house also had spots with exposed brick showing through the missing stucco.

I moved out of the door into the slight sprinkle when I heard Colin coming back down the stairs behind me. The two cops—the bigger one was Schroeder, the other Mills—gratefully took the coffee mugs from Colin. As we turned to go back inside and leave them to the crime scene, I said, "I'll leave this door unlocked so you can get out of the storm when it gets bad again."

"We'll ring the bell before we come up to interview you, or when the detectives get here," Schroeder said, nodding. "Thanks for the coffee."

"Thanks for coming out in the middle of a hurricane," Colin replied, giving him a fist bump.

I trudged back up the stairs and heard Colin close the door. My quads complained. How many times had I already gone up and down these stairs? More cardio at the gym, I decided when I reached the top with relief.

One thing I didn't like about getting older was how quickly my body reacted to lack of exercise. I wasn't fond of the soreness and stiffness, either.

I woke the television up with the remote as the boys joined me in the living room. I hoped Hester wouldn't do the same thing Isaac had, back in 2012. Isaac had parked over the city and didn't move for over twenty-four hours. Having to ride out a hurricane was bad enough on its own, but to have it last over a day? That had been *awful*. We hadn't evacuated then, either. The power had lasted maybe about an hour into the storm before going out. We just sat there, our hurricane lamps lit, listening to the howling wind and torrential rain in the flickering gaslight. Frank had been a nervous wreck the entire time. I don't remember *why* we didn't go that time, just that I regretted it. I decided then we'd never ride another one out.

Yet here we were, riding out another one.

The thing with hurricanes was they weren't something you could ever get used to. Every hurricane was different: They followed different paths, some moved faster than others, some were heavy with rain, while others caused more wind damage. They wobbled and weaved and shifted and turned and did unexpected things on their way to landfall once they made it into the warm bathtub that was the Gulf of Mexico. The warm water fed them, made them bigger and more dangerous. Several literally swung east at the last possible moment and missed the city with the eye wall.

You hear me, Hester? No hovering!

I looked up at the roof and mentally shook my fist.

But at least our power was still on.

The clock on the microwave read 8:15. I'd only been awake for a little more than an hour?

Hurricanes really messed with the space-time continuum.

I switched from the local channel to The Weather Channel. Jim Cantore wasn't on camera now—it was some barely recognizable young man in a rain slicker on Grand Isle. The camera lens was polka-dotted with beads of water, and the wind was blowing so hard into his microphone he could barely be heard over it. The conditions looked terrible. He was having a hard time keeping his balance, and it looked like he was standing on top of the big seawall there. The waves out in the Gulf looked enormous and dangerous. Storm surge had already pushed water up onto the beach. As I watched, a wave crashed against the levee itself, spraying him with water. "They're telling us we need to get out now," he yelled over the wind, "before the water cuts off the road out!"

They cut back to the studio, the anchor advising him to stay safe out there.

Grand Isle was a barrier island in Jefferson Parish—basically the last gasp of land between Barataria Bay and the Gulf. It's small, and about a two-hour drive south of the city. Grand Isle had year-round residents, of course, but the island also had beach houses for some New Orleanians to escape the abusive summers and fish. Being a low-lying barrier island, hurricanes were never kind to Grand Isle. Sometimes a storm surge would crash over the entire island, taking almost everything with it as it washed back out, leaving behind a foot of salt water for a couple of days before it all finally receded. Papa Bradley had a place out there for years, but after it was destroyed yet again by Hurricane Gustav in 2008, he sold the land. Now he and Mamaw Bradley had their beach home in Destin, over the state line in Florida.

I started reaching for the blunt from last night in the ashtray on the coffee table.

That's what I usually did to relieve my nerves while riding out a storm—got good and baked. It's never failed me yet, and I bet everyone awake at the main house was drinking either Bloody Marys or mimosas. Getting drunk was also a popular hurricane pastime, but why risk a hangover when you could just smoke weed? I imagine some people were having hurricane parties, but that always seemed like tempting fate to me. Nah, my way of getting through was better.

It *was* early in the morning, and Venus and Blaine *were* on their way…

And this time, I wanted nothing to do with this murder. Let them do their jobs and I'd stay out of their way. I sparked the joint and took a couple of quick hits, letting the calm spread through my body. Yes, much better, I thought, pinching it out and spraying Febreze.

Maybe I could suggest we armchair detective the case? That would keep Frank's mind occupied and off the storm.

Maybe after the storm passed…?

No.

I pushed that thought right out of my mind.

But if the boys or the family were in danger…

Enough.

I reached for the cigar box with my tarot cards and started shuffling. I didn't like to mess with the cards before hurricanes because I was afraid of what I might see. But if I just asked about Kristin's murder, my gift wouldn't show me something terrible, right?

I spread the cards, looked them over, and sighed.

Meaningless.

My so-called gift never worked when I needed it to…but maybe that meant we weren't in any danger. I scooped the cards up and put them back in their box as Frank walked into the kitchen to make another cup of coffee.

"Where've you been?" I asked as I switched the television back to Lisette Reynolds.

She was standing in front of a constantly moving satellite map with a massive rounded white splotch just off the southern coast of the Louisiana shore. "Right now, Hester is not moving other than her rotational spin." Her eyes were so wide open that if she sneezed, they'd pop right out. "But this wind shear we were seeing in the upper atmosphere that was keeping the storm from getting bigger is now moving east without the storm." She was too professional to gulp, but she looked like she wanted to. "Which means we don't know if the storm will intensify as it stays out over the water. But right now, Hester is still a Category 2, and the storm surge we were seeing is holding steady. That should be the case until she starts moving again."

"I took a shower," Frank replied. He was wearing a different ratty pair of gray sweats, and his stubbly chest hair looked wet and dark. He looked a little pale to me.

"Is she saying it could get stronger?" Colin plopped down next to me on the couch. "Leave it to you to stumble over a corpse during a hurricane." He squeezed my leg with his big warm calloused hand.

"It's not *my* fault," I replied automatically. He and Frank teased me mercilessly. The corpse thing was a joke everyone in my family loved to join in on when we're all together.

It's a wonder I'm not in a straitjacket.

A thought I've had any number of times in my life.

If anything, I was the world's most reluctant detective. Sure, we technically *did* have a detective agency licensed by the state, but we didn't go looking for clients. We didn't need the money. We did have an office we rented over on Frenchmen Street for a few months before Hurricane Katrina, but the only work we ever got was when Storm threw us some insurance fraud investigations from his law firm. The murders were just me stumbling over bodies, time after time after time. Nope, the murders were never paying gigs, which was just as well. It's not like I was Sherlock Holmes or anything. Sometimes the cards told me a way to go or helped redirect my thinking, but even when I went to the other realm and talked to the Goddess—well, she's always so obscure I never understood what help she gave me until later.

I just got lucky a lot.

Which was really the story of my entire life, wasn't it?

I must have been born under a lucky star or something.

"I hate thinking about Venus and Blaine out in this weather," Frank said, sitting down on my other side. "But I'd hate being the one who dragged them out in this weather more." He and Colin reached in front of me to clink their mugs together.

They're so lucky the sex is amazing.

"I just assumed they wouldn't come out, honestly," I replied, resisting the urge to knock their heads together. "Isn't that why the state and city make all those announcements about no one coming to rescue you if you don't leave? To keep them safe?"

"Murder is a little bit different." Frank reached for the remote and flipped it back to The Weather Channel. "As it is, the crime scene is pretty much wrecked already, which is a lucky break for the killer. Who knows how much evidence got washed away? And having that branch land on her wasn't much help—although they'll be able to tell what injuries were pre- and post-mortem. I just hope they're able to get enough evidence to catch whoever did it."

"I just can't wrap my mind around it," I replied as Scooter hopped into my lap and started making biscuits. He was also purring, which called for some head and under-the-chin scratches. After a few moments of this, he curled up and closed his eyes, exhaling in an exhausted sigh. He really was adorable. "Why would someone want to kill a home care nurse? Did you find anything on her social media?"

"No." Colin frowned, waking up his laptop by touching the space bar. "There really wasn't very much about her—she has social media accounts, but they look like placeholders to me, like she put them up in case someone went looking for them." He turned the laptop around. Kristin's Facebook page was on his screen. The profile picture was her, beaming at the camera and wearing no makeup, like I remembered. The background image was a shot of New Orleans from the air, at night—the lights running across the lake on the causeway meant it was probably taken from an airplane window on final descent into the airport. One hundred and thirteen friends, no mutuals with Colin at any rate. The last time something had been posted had been last year. It also said she was forty-two, close to my age.

Did I look that old? I wondered like I always do when I see a picture of someone close to my age. I didn't feel like I was in my forties.

I didn't think I looked like I did, either. But there's no delusion like self-delusion, right?

"It looks to me like she made social media accounts when she was looking for work," Colin went on. "Her Facebook page was only created last December, and all of her accounts—Twitter, LinkedIn, everything—were also created on the same day." He shrugged. "When I've run across this before, it usually means the person had accounts already but scrubbed them all to hide things from potential employers. It probably doesn't mean anything, it's getting more and more common."

"Like how kids have a generic account their family can see and then create another one with their first and middle names?" Frank replied. We'd all learned that trick when Taylor moved in with us.

"I'll try the Wayback Machine and see if I can find anything, but like I said, it's probably nothing." Colin rubbed his chin. "Maybe...maybe we're looking at this wrong."

"What do you mean?" I asked.

"What if Kristin wasn't the murderer's *real* target?" Colin blew out his breath and had an odd look on his face.

"You think it was something random?" Frank scowled. "Before a hurricane? Colin, get real."

"No, not something random," Colin replied, staring at his screen and drumming his fingers on the table. "Although if it wasn't for the weather, and that everyone in town has known a storm was possible all week, we might have thought she got mugged. But her car isn't here—"

"Unless it's at the dower house," I pointed out.

"Unless it's there, yes, but if it's not?" He whistled. "How did she get here? She lives in Kenner. I doubt United is open, and I can't believe anyone was driving for Lyft earlier this morning, can you?"

I opened the app on my phone. The map showed no cars, and there was a message: *For the safety of our drivers we will not be accepting rides until after Hester. Please check back with us!* I held it up for them to see. "I don't know when they shut down, but you never know. I'm sure someone in the city was driving until they did. But if her car's not here, someone had to drive her here, alive or dead. And if that's the case, why?"

"Maybe she had car trouble," Frank surmised. "And she might not have been killed here, either."

I replied, "But why would anyone go to that much trouble

to get rid of her body? I mean, when you think about it, why *here*? Unless it was to bring attention—"

"To the family," Frank finished.

"Or us," Colin said. "I mean, the body was right outside the garage door. Who else are the cops going to want to talk to besides all of us?"

A silence descended over the room. We sat there, listening to the wind starting to pick up and the rustling of branches rubbing against each other in the wind.

"And it may not have anything to do with any of us." Colin broke the silence. "Who knows? Maybe she has a sordid life none of us knows anything about. Maybe she's a blackmailer, maybe she's having an affair with a married man, who knows?" He grinned. "All I know is that this time, it's not me. I left Blackledge, and that is over and done with. It's got nothing to do with me!" He jumped to his feet and raised his hands above his head, revealing the deep hollows of his armpits.

I couldn't help but laugh. How many times had something from Colin's international man of mystery world put all of us in danger?

"Scotty has almost as many enemies as you." Frank joined in on the teasing. "Have any of those people you put away all those years ago gotten out of prison?"

It never occurred to me before. But yeah, it had been almost fifteen years since that gang of white supremacists went to jail. The ringleaders and others that could be connected to their acts of terror had gotten lengthy sentences for all their charges, and the sentences weren't concurrent. No, Willy Perkins wouldn't be getting out of jail until long after I was buried. But some of the others had gotten lighter sentences for turning state's evidence.

I hoped they were keeping their noses clean and keeping far away from me.

But Colin was still in an awkward place with us. When the

three of us had embarked on the adventure of being in what people now call a throuple (I like to think people invented the term to describe us, because of course *everything* is about me), we'd promised each other complete and total honesty. It was the only way our relationship could possibly work. And then he'd lied to us—and my family—about something important. He hadn't had a choice—it had to do with his job, and he said it was the only way he could keep us safe. We worked through all of that and forgave him. Then I came home from a party to find him bleeding and standing over a dead body in our living room. Things got worse when I allowed him to convince me to help him get rid of the body. Yes, I became an accessory after the fact, interfered with a criminal investigation, and who knows what other laws I'd broken. But the guy *was* a Russian agent, and since he'd found us, we didn't know if we were safe from other people who might want revenge on Colin for things he'd done when he was with Blackledge.

And no, I didn't want to know the things he did while working for them, either.

Some things were better left unsaid.

I hated that I still had doubts about whether he could be trusted or not. Frank, with twenty years in the FBI, was more trusting than me.

And what did that say about me?

Something I'd rather not face, I think.

"Well"—I hesitated before plunging on—"I don't think it's Colin's past, and I don't think it's yours from the FBI—so maybe it could be someone out for revenge against me, but I don't see it. Why now? But Papa Diderot probably has made enemies over the course of his life, too." I shook my head. "But that doesn't make sense either. Why kill Kristin to bring attention to us, or the family? And we don't know enough about Kristin. Too many unknowns, and besides…" I took a deep breath and exhaled. "It's not our case. Let's just let Venus and Blaine handle it for once. This time." My voice took on a pleading note I wasn't happy to hear.

"Well, there's no reason we can't brainstorm the case to keep us occupied during the storm," Frank pointed out. "I'm not suggesting we go interview people or anything—we can't until after the storm, anyway. But what can it hurt to just snoop around a bit online, come up with some theories? Could be fun. And we could lose power at any minute and lose the internet..."

I loved when my plans came together without me having to do anything.

The shutters on the roadside windows of the apartment started flashing blue, meaning another police vehicle had pulled up without us hearing it. No need to use sirens when the roads were clear, I figured. I walked over to the back windows and pulled the curtains back. The Crime Lab vehicle was parked below, and Venus and Blaine were getting out of her black Range Rover. "It's Blaine and Venus," I called back to them. "I'm going to head down—"

The entire room went white as lightning cracked very close by, and the thunder that followed almost immediately was deafening, like someone downstairs had fired a cannon. Another long gust of wind roared around the building, whistling as it felt its way around the building, looking for ways to get inside and rattling the chimney pots. Once it died down, a deluge of rain started pouring down. It sounded like someone had turned on a shower on the roof. The lights blinked a couple of times but stayed on.

"Maybe I'll just stay up here and wait for them to come up," I said, sitting back down on the couch and pulling a wool blanket around me. It was getting colder, which meant the temperature outside was dropping.

"Okay," I went on. "What we do know is that Kristin Pitre was hired to be the primary home care nurse for Aunt

Erica, with others coming in at night. I think I remember Maman saying that her doctor made the arrangements for the home health care. So, Aunt Erica probably didn't even meet the woman before she started working for her." Aunt Erica had no problems with firing anyone. She was that horrible type of rich white woman who enjoyed being mean to people. My mother had a natural mothering tendency she applied to stray animals and people. She was always helping young queer people find jobs and homes and slipping them some cash and weed to get them by from time to time. Emily Hunter was a young lesbian who'd come to New Orleans for Carnival and never left. Mom hired her to work at their tobacco shop, the Devil's Weed, and helped her find a place to live farther down Royal Street. Emily was now singing lead for a bluesy rock band—her voice and range were amazing—and traveling the country, always dropping by Mom's whenever Emily was in town and always sending postcards from the road, which Mom kept on the refrigerator.

Mom was like Maman that way. Maman always tried to make anyone she employed feel like they were a part of the family. Sure, they were paid, but Maman treated them with respect, paid them well, and did things like send their kids to college.

Aunt Erica didn't get that gene.

Mom told me once she refused to go to restaurants with Erica, because of the way Erica treated waitstaff. Mom always says you can tell what kind of person someone is by how they treat service personnel, and she's right. Lowballing on the tip, being a pain in the ass, sending food back, berating the waiter? "It's embarrassing," Mom would say with a shake of her head. "She has so much, so why she behaves like she's better than other people instead of just being grateful for what she has is a mystery to me. We weren't raised to be assholes, you know."

Which was why Aunt Erica had to move out of her impressive apartment on St. Charles Avenue. There was no one in the family willing to go stay with her while she convalesced, and she was afraid to be at—as she put it—the mercy of nurses she didn't know. So there she was in the dower house. Mom would convalesce at home in the Quarter, Dad waiting on her hand and foot, with her kids and their families dropping in to check on her all the time.

Not to mention her friends. There were times when I thought Mom and Dad knew everyone in New Orleans.

No one had come to visit Aunt Erica that I was aware of.

I liked to think I wouldn't be lonely if I was recovering from surgery.

Family in Louisiana can be complicated. We have any number of relatives we don't have much to do with—like the Haver cousins in St. Jeanne d'Arc Parish. One of our cases involved them, so I had the great joy of introducing the boys to them.

I'm still surprised they didn't leave me.

I'd have considered it if I'd been them.

"Wasn't she married a bunch of times?" Frank asked. He always paid attention to family stuff and probably knew more about my own family than I did. "If there was a bad divorce—"

Another gust of wind shook the building, the shutters pulling against their latches. That creaking noise they made when they moved in the wind was almost like fingernails on a chalkboard to me. My teeth itched, and my nerves all jangled together. The rain was still battering the roof. The lights flickered a few more times.

I moved a little closer to Frank on the couch and leaned into him. "Her last divorce was…five years ago? The one before that died and—" I sat straight up. "Oh Lord, how could I have forgotten? Colin, do a Google search on Riley Foster." There was something there, something from her past that came up recently. I'd made note of it but not really.

She'd divorced Tucker Foster in what? 2007? 2008?

The name had seemed familiar at the time, but I wasn't

paying enough attention, and it passed over me without remembering because it all happened so long ago. It was the summer of 2005 when Riley Foster threw acid in that escort's face. Apollo? Was that the name? It sounded right. It hadn't been his real name, but he'd gone by Apollo.

Colin whistled. "There's a piece here on NOLA.com from a few weeks ago." He looked over at us. "He assaulted someone and fled the country before he could be arrested. It says here that the family was working on getting a presidential pardon." He made a face. "Justice for sale, right?"

"What does that have to do with Aunt Erica?" Frank asked as the room lit up with white light before the house-rattling boom that followed.

"God, how could I have forgotten about that?" I shivered and cuddled closer to Frank's warmth. "Riley's dad was Aunt Erica's third husband, I think. She was married to him when this all went down." I felt a bit nauseous remembering it all and remembered distancing myself from the Foster family-by-marriage.

Aunt Erica had met Tucker Foster in rehab, of all places. He had a problem with sleeping pills, and she had essentially been checked in by Maman and Papa Diderot after her third drunk driving arrest. I know Papa pulled some strings down at city hall because she never spent any time in jail. They met and fell in love at rehab, and when they got out, they flew to Las Vegas to get married before his children even had a chance to meet her. She'd moved into the big Foster house down near Audubon Park, and the whole Diderot family was invited to the reception they threw for themselves in that big house. The oldest child, Davina, was engaged and was too lost in talk about her own wedding plans to be bothered with anyone else. The youngest, Tom, was hitting on every woman in the place.

Riley gave me the creeps from the moment we first met.

New Orleans is enough of a small town for me to have

heard of the Fosters, even if I'd never met them; they were part of the tangled lines and crossed wires that made up the New Orleans social scene. Riley's girlfriend seemed to just fade into the woodwork and couldn't make any conversation other than something superficial and meaningless. But Riley?

"I guess we're cousins now!" he'd said when we were introduced. He was in his mid-to-late twenties and had that slightly inbred look all society people in town seemed to share. His hair was blond, dwindling, and slicked back away from his very pale face, so pale his skin almost seemed translucent. He was handsome enough, if you liked that type, was tall and slender, but overeating and overdrinking were starting to make their presence felt in his waist. He was wearing a classic seersucker suit, and he gave me a big hug that...well, it didn't feel right to me. He held on to me too long, for one, and pressed his chest against mine harder than most men did. And when he finally let me go, his left hand brushed over my ass slightly, just enough for me to know, too nothing to say anything about because it could just be laughed off.

But I knew the type. More than I'd like to, honestly.

Closet case!

While frowned upon in New Orleans society, being gay was fine so long as you had a wife and maybe kids and a nice big house and an important name and a fat bank account. You came to an understanding with your wife, usually kept a small apartment in the Quarter or close enough to get up to whatever you got up to outside your marital bed. My dad's family had expected me, despite coming out, to follow that route and live two lives. Not for me, thank you. And their affairs were none of my business. I just knew I wasn't going to be one of their side pieces, even just once. And Riley had that vibe. Big-time.

So when he threw acid in Apollo's face, the scandal didn't surprise me. I knew Apollo, too. He'd started out as a dancer, like me, and that was how we met. He was gorgeous, no doubt.

He was tall and had olive skin and green eyes and that body. My word, that body. He moved from dancing to the occasional porn film and escorting, and he made good money. He was a very nice guy, and he was honest about what he wanted—he knew he was blessed with looks and a body, and he wanted to milk that for as long as he could before settling down with a rich man. If only he'd asked me about Riley…

Riley was jealous and possessive and didn't trust his beautiful kept boy. Certain Apollo was going to leave him, he decided to make sure no one else would want Apollo.

It was horrifying. Apollo almost died, and Riley fled the country. Everyone thought Tucker and Erica were sending him money, and it was a bit of a scandal for a while. I'd thought about visiting Apollo and seeing how he was doing but felt it might be weird because Riley was kind of a relative. I'd forgotten all this—Katrina later that summer kind of pushed all that stuff out of my mind.

Colin's phone dinged. "Venus and Blaine are on their way up."

Chapter Five

The Emperor

Authority

There was another flash of lightning, the lights flickering as another big gust roared around the house. It seemed to go on forever. It stopped just as the thunder shook the house before it could settle back.

It had kind of a *Wizard of Oz* feel I didn't like.

I didn't realize I'd been clenching my fists until the only sound was the endless drenching rain. I glanced over at Frank, but other than the nerve in his jaw twitching, he seemed okay.

I could tell the door downstairs had opened. I heard the murmur of voices and footsteps, and the door closed again with a loud thud.

I snapped out of the unease and checked around the living room. I grabbed the ashtray holding the roaches and the half joint I'd just smoked, and the cigar box I keep the weed in with the other hand, shoving everything under the sofa. I sprayed some more Febreze to be on the safe side and lit some vanilla candles. Venus and Blaine had probably smelled the smoke in the apartment before, and I wasn't always the best about hiding everything. They probably wouldn't care, but why put their ethics on the line?

At least be respectful of their jobs, right?

On the other hand, they've also been to Mom and Dad's, where you could get high scraping the resin off their walls. I also closed our laptops—no sense letting them see what we were researching. We weren't getting involved in their case as anything other than an intellectual exercise.

Besides, their real investigation wouldn't get started until after the hurricane anyway.

I went to meet them at the top of the stairs. They were both wearing their official NOPD yellow rain slickers. Every step shook more water from the slick yellow coverings. I took those coats and hung them in our bathroom, draping them over the shower curtain rod to drip into the tub. When I rejoined everyone, Venus and Blaine were both seated in the reclining chairs in the living room, drinking coffee and looking a bit frazzled.

"Y'all okay?" I asked, sitting down on the couch and picking up my own lukewarm coffee. "Sorry to get you out here on such a bad day."

It's been close to about fifteen years since Venus and Blaine responded to my 911 call during Southern Decadence when I came home from a night of dancing on the bar to find a dead body outside the front gate. That was also the *first* time I stumbled over a dead body. It took them a few years and a few more dead bodies to warm up to me—well, *us*. I was still not sure they'd warmed up all the way, but they didn't seem to get as mad as they used to when me and the boys interfered with their murder investigations. Venus was tall and lean, all sinew and tendon and muscle fibers. She'd gone to college on a basketball scholarship before returning to New Orleans and joining the force. Her two daughters were also basketball stars in college, and she had several grandchildren now. Her face was as unlined as it was when I first laid eyes on her. She tended to wear gray or black suits with matching skirts or pants, and stylish but serviceable heels that weren't too high to run in, should she need to. She always kept her hair cropped close to her skull, but I could see more gray hair in the stubble than the last time I'd seen her. She'd mentioned thinking about retiring soon.

Which was great for her, but what would that mean for us?

Don't get me wrong. I know that's selfish.

She'd worked hard for a long time, and it wasn't easy to make it up the ranks as the first Black woman detective in a slowly integrating police force. She'd been very good to us, like I said. She was good to us even when she was more annoyed by us.

Or maybe, just maybe, I'd stop falling over bodies once she retired. I can't imagine her replacement would be willing to put up with me and the boys the way she had.

"You know, when the dispatcher told us the name of the person who called in a dead body, I wasn't even surprised," Blaine said with a laugh and eye roll. "A dead body in a hurricane? It had to be you guys."

Blaine was a good-looking man in his midforties, close to my age. We were also close to the same height. But Blaine had olive skin, bluish-black hair, and dark blue sapphire eyes. Like me, Blaine was a gay son of New Orleans society. We'd never crossed paths growing up, though—Mom and Dad never sent me to the grueling society classes where I'd learn how to dance and be a gentleman. We'd gone to different high schools. I never went to Carnival balls so had never seen him at any of those. *Crescent City* magazine did a feature on him once, around ten years ago or so. I hadn't known he was the first openly gay detective in the NOPD or how hard he'd worked to make the NOPD more inclusive of queer officers.

With his easygoing attitude, I'd have never guessed he was an activist.

Of course, I'd seen him in the bars and around the Quarter before we did meet. He wasn't out all the time, but he could be spotted on the dance floor drenched in sweat from time to time. He was noticeable. He had a great body he clearly kept up with regular workouts. His biceps were big, his shoulders wide, and his waist narrow. Whenever he costumed, he wore very little. There was some dark hair in the center of his chest, and he didn't shave his armpits, either. With his square jaw, deep dimples, and eyes that sparkled when he smiled, he was drop dead gorgeous. He used to keep his hair short enough so it wouldn't curl, but now that he had some gray coming in, he was letting the curls grow out. His thick mop of bluish-black curls framed his face to a better effect.

He was totally my type—he and Colin could pass as brothers if you didn't look closely enough. We weren't entirely sure we hadn't slept together years ago on some hot frantic night with lots of drugs and alcohol coursing through our veins. Chances were we probably had, since I'd been an unabashed and unashamed slut when I was single. It was a shame I couldn't remember it. He'd been married to an art gallery owner for several decades, living with him on Coliseum Square in the lower Garden District. His husband, whose name I couldn't remember, had passed away last winter. The gallery on Royal Street was still there, though, not far from Mom and Dad's place.

"I got to say, though, guys, you're definitely moving up in the world." Blaine laughed. "Although this place doesn't seem as nice as your place in the Quarter. When can you move back?"

"We're hoping by the end of the month," Frank replied.

"We were supposed to be back by July first," Colin added.

Venus shook her head. "Y'all have certainly lived here long enough to know nothing ever finishes when it's supposed to, let alone construction work." A smile hinted at the corner of her lips. She pulled out a notepad from her inner jacket pocket and made a face. "I was kind of hoping I'd retire before we got hit again. I hate hurricanes."

"It sucks having to be on duty," I said. No one ever thought about first responders when it came to hurricanes. No, everyone just focused on themselves and getting on the road as quickly as they could. Whenever there's a mandatory evacuation order, people staying were always warned they were on their own until the storm was past.

I'd never thought about it until Hurricane Katrina. I just figured they left, too.

But when the federally funded and maintained levees failed and flooded the city in the storm's wake, the entire New Orleans Police Department completely failed in front of the entire country. Rumors flew that it was the cops who'd looted Sewell Cadillac, taking all the cars on the lot. There was no way for anyone to communicate, there was no leadership or worst-case plan, so the city descended into lawlessness and crime in the name of survival. The lack of a police presence hadn't helped.

Our police department had never had the best reputation. They'd gone on strike decades ago, right before Carnival, thinking that the city would meet their demands. Instead, the city canceled Mardi Gras and broke the strike. The city turned against its police officers, and their low pay and bad conditions led to even more corruption than was already there. Crime got bad here after the blows delivered by the explosion of the crack epidemic and the Big Oil bust, and white flight to the suburbs in the wake of desegregation had hollowed out the city's tax base by the 1980s. And it got worse from there. There was a scandal in the late 1990s where some corrupt cops put out a hit on a complaining witness in a police brutality case, but undercover Feds got it all on tape. The woman was murdered, and the scandal led to some big reforms and an overhaul of the force. Things had been getting better until Katrina took them a giant step backward.

There hadn't been a national scandal about the NOPD since Katrina—but you never knew. Maybe the crooked cops were better at being crooked and were getting away with it.

After Katrina, there had been another big push to rid the police department of bad characters and corrupt crooks in uniform. Out-of-towners were easily terrified by reading the comments section beneath articles about New Orleans—a combination of horror stories and replies from locals, trying to be helpful, who warned them about where not to go. This didn't give our tourists the best impression of how safe the city was or wasn't.

Complaining about the cops and crime were more popular conversational topics here than the weather. Potholes, though, would always be the most popular.

One good thing to come out of Katrina was that the role of the NOPD during storms hitting the city became better defined. They were all at work, responding to calls as quickly and safely as possible given storm conditions, and we all chose to believe there was a plan in place should something like catastrophic levee failure—especially of levees built and maintained by the Army Corps of Engineers—happen. Hopefully, we'd never see anything like the chaos after Katrina again.

Fortunately, we hadn't had a repeat of a levee failure since then.

"That's why we responded to your call." Blaine sipped his coffee. "Knowing you as well as we do, it's easier for us—and besides, we couldn't do that to our colleagues—so we jumped on the grenade." He, too, pulled a notepad from his shirt pocket. "And I want to swing by my mom's farther uptown and check in on her. Two birds, one stone." He gave me a grin that would have made my knees weak twenty years ago if I'd seen it in a bar.

Hell, it would now if I didn't know him so well. Yes, he was very hot and sexy. He looked great shirtless and slick with sweat. It would be like fucking...not a *brother*, but maybe a cousin?

"Yeah, well, glad it's y'all who answered, but sorry you had to," I replied, sitting down in one of the easy chairs. My coffee had gotten cold. "Any news on the storm? Has it shifted more to the east?"

"Well, I hate to break it to you all," Venus drawled slowly, "but looks like good ole Hester has rotated around and is heading back offshore. But don't worry—she's coming back, of course. Maybe a few hours' delay in the storm getting here, but there are still plenty of goddamned bands coming in. The Hurricane Center is concerned that it'll pick up size and strength because the Gulf water is so warm. It may come back in as a 2."

I whistled. A Category 2 was still bad.

My biggest fear since Katrina, to be honest, was that one day some storm would brew up and grow to monster size so quickly we wouldn't have time to get out of town.

It's never fun riding out a storm of any size.

I realized I was clenching my fists again.

"So, we probably shouldn't be keeping you out," Frank said. "Do you want to talk to us individually, or—"

Venus and Blaine exchanged a glance. "Well"—Venus cleared her throat—"it's not procedure to interview you all together, but..." She sighed. "If you needed to come up with a cover story, you certainly have had plenty of time. I know you all well enough by now to know you wouldn't make a mistake and you wouldn't trip up, but I also don't think you suddenly turned and became murderers, either." She raised an eyebrow. "Do any of you have a reason to kill Nurse Kristin Pitre?"

"Of course not," I replied, although a little nagging voice in the back of my head whispered insidiously *You don't know that* Colin *didn't*...but dismissed it with a quick shake of my head. I've always hated that little voice. "I barely knew her at all. She was hired—"

"You don't bother getting to know the help?" Blaine interrupted me with a sly smile and a wink.

I blew a raspberry at him. "Ha ha ha, oh so witty. Why you aren't writing jokes for Kathy Griffin remains a mystery to this day."

"Ignore him." Venus gave Blaine a stern look. "She was hired?"

"She was the primary home health care worker for my Aunt Erica."

"Erica?"

"Erica Diderot. Mom's younger sister. She broke her hip about a month ago."

"She's staying here?" Venus raised her eyebrows.

I nodded. "Erica lives by herself, and she needed someone to come in. My grandmother didn't like the idea of her being alone at home, so moved her into the dower house for the duration." Both Venus and Blaine nodded.

"Walk us through this morning," Venus prodded.

I looked at Frank, who said, "I was up first. I woke up around six o'clock and couldn't fall back asleep. I got up, made some coffee, checked on the storm path, and that's about it. Scotty got up around seven, and we heard a loud crash from the street side"—he gestured in that direction—"which also woke up Colin. Scotty went down to see what it was."

"And is that when you found the body?" That was Blaine, scribbling in his notepad.

"Yes." I took up the story. "At first, I thought the noise had been the branch hitting the garage door, but then I saw, well, the body underneath it. I thought she might need help, but when I got to her, her lips were blue and her face...well, she looked dead." I hesitated. "I think she'd been there for a while."

Frank agreed, adding, "The body was cold, her face was bluish, and her lips purple. She'd been out there long enough for the body to get cold—and it was super humid last night."

"It was," Venus agreed. "The heat last night would have delayed rigor for a while. Was she supposed to come into work today?"

"Maman—Mrs. Diderot—didn't want Erica left down at the dower house during the storm in case she lost power.

What if Kristin couldn't come in?" Frank said. "And if the power went out…So we moved Erica up to the main house." He frowned, wrinkling his forehead. "Kristin wasn't much help, now that I think about it. She didn't help with the move at all or try to keep Erica comfortable, which wasn't easy. Erica complained all the way to the main house." He made a face. I knew he was thinking: piece of work.

I know I was.

"Kristin didn't think it was even necessary to move her up to the house," Colin said. "Frank, you weren't there when we talked it over. Kristin insisted that it wasn't necessary because she was planning on coming to work this morning. She said she could leave before the storm came in, and she'd just plan on staying if things got too bad for her to go home after."

"She wanted to come to work?" Venus replied. "During a hurricane?"

"She's a nurse," Frank added. "Maybe nurses view these things differently. I know the hospitals don't close."

"It's not the same thing." I shook my head. "I think it's weird. She wasn't abandoning her patient. The main house is full of people."

"Maman and Papa didn't want to let her come," Colin answered. "She kept insisting she didn't mind, it wasn't an inconvenience, and she'd just come in early." He scratched his head. "I know both Papa and Maman told her there wasn't a need, but she said she'd pack a bag just in case, and she wouldn't feel right abandoning her patient for a storm." He held up his hands. "I kind of admired the dedication, to be honest. Aunt Erica is a handful. I'd jump at any excuse to not have to deal with her!"

I continued, "When I was up at the main house this morning, Nora—the housekeeper—told me Kristin was supposed to call her if she was coming in. She never heard from her, so she thought she wasn't coming." I looked over at Colin. He wasn't wrong about Erica.

He winked. "I've spent some time with your aunt since we moved in here. She's…interesting." He made a face. "Her values and beliefs are, well, kind of warped? It's hard to believe Mom is her sister." He mock-shuddered. "I can see why Mom doesn't like her."

"They've never been close," I explained with a wave of my hand. Our family dramas weren't important.

"What do you mean *interesting*?" Venus said, like I hadn't said anything, and jotted down some notes in her pad. "Something you noticed, or just felt?"

It used to bug me that Venus took Frank and Colin more seriously than she did me. She *always* deferred to them, like I wasn't there. I mean, sure, I get it. I never graduated from college, and when she met me, all she saw was a go-go boy in gay bars who shook his butt for dollars in a thong. Frank had been in the FBI when she met him. She also knew Colin was ex-Mossad (but not that he'd been Blackledge—no one in New Orleans, not even family, knew that).

But I was the one who seemed to either catch the killer or figure out who it was, way more times than either of them. I got over her attitude with the passage of time, recognizing (with the help of my therapist) that being talked down to, or not taken seriously, was a trigger for me. No one had taken me seriously when I was younger. Well, my parents always did, but the rest of the family? Storm still treated me like I was his bratty little brother, teasing me mercilessly. Rain was better about it now than when we were kids, but she'd join in on the family dogpiles still from time to time. It was also amazing how many people thought someone who looked like me and used to be a go-go boy slash personal trainer must be a complete idiot. It was always a struggle for me to get anyone to take me seriously.

Besides my parents. They didn't count.

Now? I kind of preferred being underestimated. You

wanted to think I was just some airhead gym queen who couldn't add or subtract anything unless it was calculating the correct ingredients of a protein shake to the nearest milligram?

Underestimate me at your own peril, *bitch*.

"We did some checking on your victim after we got the call," Blaine said. "A quick look into her didn't...well, her background didn't seem to turn up any reason for anyone to kill her. Nothing *interesting*."

"Things generally don't in a cursory search," Venus added. "Is there anything going on with you guys we need to know about?"

It was a fair question, and I appreciated the discretion of her phrasing. "Not a thing." I shrugged. "As for the rest of the family...no more than usual, I guess. I mean, no one's said anything to me about it. You'll have to ask them."

"Those bruises on her neck—they weren't there yesterday?"

Both Frank and Colin said no.

Venus looked up from her pad. "Was there any reason she'd be wandering around outside your house at night?"

"You think she was out wandering the streets in the middle of the night and just happened to run into a psycho killer?" I shook my head. "That's a stretch, especially on a rainy night before a hurricane hits."

"He doesn't have to be a psycho," Colin pointed out.

"There could be all kinds of things in her private life—or her past professional life—that we don't know," Frank replied. "Yet, anyway."

"Um, maybe we shouldn't be brainstorming in front of them?" I held up my hands. Out of the corner of my eye, I could see Venus fighting a smile. "They're here to interrogate us, not talk to us about the case."

Blaine choked back a laugh and smiled at me. God, he

had the hottest smile. I used to think he was flirting with me, which was flattering but made me feel a little awkward. But I'd also noticed he flirted with everyone, male or female. It was just his nature.

And who didn't like being flirted with by a man who looked like that?

"Actually," Venus said, accepting another cup of coffee from Frank. "I'd be curious to hear your theories—*after* we've interviewed you."

"What else do you want to know?" I asked, crossing my legs and leaning back into the couch. "After we found the body and called you, I went back over to the main house—"

"In the storm," Frank interrupted.

"It was between bands," I retorted. "I'm not crazy. That's when I talked to Nora, and she told me what she and Kristin had worked out about this morning. I talked to my aunt a little bit, too, but didn't get anywhere."

"You're lucky you got out of there alive," Colin muttered.

"What does that mean?" Venus asked quickly, sitting forward with interest.

Colin looked stricken. "Oh, nothing..." He looked at me for help.

"Colin doesn't want to talk shit about my aunt, but she's my aunt, honey—I've known what she's like since I was a kid." I half laughed. "And I know you've heard Mom talk shit about her before."

"But she's your fami—"

"You're also part of the family," I cut in firmly. "What did she do?"

Colin exhaled. "Let's just say she doesn't hide her homophobia very well."

"Oh, *that*," I replied. "I'm sorry about that, babe. She wasn't always like that." I exhaled and touched his leg. "I mean, she's always been horrible, but she was never homophobic until that whole mess with her stepson Riley Foster…Oh, that's right. I forget you weren't here that summer."

"Riley Foster?" Venus and Blaine looked at each other and back at me. "The Riley Foster whose family is working on getting him a pardon so he can come home?"

"One and the same." I turned to Colin and explained what had happened with Riley and Apollo. "I always believed she was sending him money after he fled the country, but of course no one could ever prove it. She was attached to him for whatever reason. When Riley's dad divorced her, she became very bitter. That's when she started with the homophobia. I think, somehow, she blamed what Riley did for the divorce. It's insane, but that's my aunt." I sighed. "Nothing is ever her fault."

"There are rumors he's already come back to New Orleans, you know," Venus said quietly, writing in her notepad.

"It's amazing how anyone can just buy a pardon these days," Frank said bitterly. "He threw acid in someone's face, flees the country, and because his father knows a guy who knows a guy who knows a guy, pardoned." Twenty years as a Fed dedicated to justice left a mark.

Venus looked up from her pad. "We also can't rule out that you guys are the real target, either. Her body was outside your house, and you've made your share of enemies over the years. Hasn't it ever occurred to you someone might come back after you?"

I'd never thought about it before this morning. They all wound up in jail for murder and their other crimes, so I never gave them a second thought. My worry had always been someone from Colin's past showing up with a loaded AK-47 and a taste for revenge. His security had been breached last December (it's a long story) but it's also why we'd turned the Decatur Street house into as much of a secured fortress as we could.

The renovation would make it even more secure.

But there's no such thing as a completely secure house, just like there's no such thing as an unsinkable ship.

Venus waved her hand around. "This place isn't as secure as your actual home, is it? And it might take a while for that information to get around."

I'd just assumed anyone looking for us *there* wouldn't know to look for us *here*.

There were at least two racist homophobic groups whose plans I'd foiled. Not all the gang members had gone to prison.

And the dark powers of hatred and bigotry were rising again, not just in Louisiana but across the country. Taylor raged about the transphobia and racism that seemed to have bubbled up all over again the last few years. Going to Tulane was radicalizing a kid who not that long ago was in the pews of the Church of Christ every Sunday morning and evening, certain that if he ever acted on his lusts and urges for other young men he'd go straight to hell and would lose everything he cared about. He wasn't wrong. He'd fallen in love with a young French waiter when he was doing a semester abroad in France, and his parents had cut him off immediately. That's when he'd come to live with us and become a part of our family.

"You haven't...um...heard anything, have you?" My voice sounded shakier than I felt.

Venus smirked. "Always a drama queen. No, we haven't heard anything, but we can check in on some of the people you helped put behind bars, see what we can find out." She typed expertly on her phone with her thumbs, something I couldn't do.

"We also don't know how she got here," I remembered. "We didn't see her car parked anywhere on the street when we were out there. It just doesn't make sense that she'd be outside our place. Why was she here so early when she never got here before eight? Why didn't she call Nora, like she said she was going to?"

Blaine asked, "Where did she usually park?"

"She always parked at the dower house," Colin said.

"There's a little parking area behind the main house, just back by the dower house," I explained to Venus and Blaine. "I should have thought to check if her car was there when I was at the main house." Main house, dower house, carriage house—I hoped Venus and Blaine were keeping track because even I was getting confused. I'd never thought about my grandparents having too many buildings on their property. "I was in a hurry because it was starting to rain and get windy again, and I wanted to get back over here before things got bad again with the next band—and I thought it was better to get back here and wait for you to show up."

"So, you've had no threats, not noticed anyone suspicious hanging around? Haven't gotten yourselves mixed up in something you're not sure how to tell us about?" Venus took another swig from her coffee.

"No, ma'am." We always paid attention to our surroundings. I guess my mind had protected me from thinking about all the criminals who wanted to get even with *me*. I felt sure Colin had contacted his old boss at Blackledge as soon as he was alone after we found Kristin, either by phone or email. Anytime someone died around us, Colin worried it was Blackledge-related in some way.

We were never going to be able to completely relax.

And then I remembered the slip of paper in her hand. "Hang on for a second," I said, heading back down to my room to retrieve the sweats I'd originally worn. I handed it to Venus, who frowned as I explained where I'd found it.

"You took something from my crime scene?" she said, her eyes narrowing.

"I was worried it would, you know, get ruined by the rain."

"*Hill*," she said, still frowning.

"I don't know what it means."

She dropped it into an evidence bag, making notes on it with her Sharpie. She dropped the baggie into her bag. "Well, I guess we should head up to the main house." Venus put her cup down. "Thank you for the coffee."

I could still hear the rain pelting the ceiling and the wind whipping around the building. It was a mournful sound, one that easily got under my skin in no time. The wind was always the worst part of riding out a storm for me.

On the television, Jim Cantore had retreated from Grand Isle and was heading for another port in the storm to report from. A Category 2 would probably level the entire island again.

"Let me get your coats," Colin said, getting up and heading for the back stairs.

"I'll go over there with you," I said as I stood up. I was getting a little antsy, and that wind sound…I'd be happy to get away from that for a little while.

I picked up my phone and shoved it into my sweatpants pocket. I found a pair of beach sandals and slipped them on, buckling them around my ankles—better than the flip-flops.

There was a strong gust of wind that lasted for about twenty seconds, whistling around the carriage house like a banshee, followed by a torrential downpour.

The lights blinked, came back on, flickered, and went dead.

Chapter Six

Queen of Swords, Reversed

A sly and deceitful woman

The silence in our now gloomy home lasted only a few seconds before there was a chorus of moans and groans. Glows appeared around the room as everyone woke up their phones.

"Internet's gone," Colin announced glumly. "No cell service, either."

I often thought about how spoiled we all were by electricity, but only when it went out. Especially in the summer. The cloud cover was keeping the temperatures down, but even so, it wouldn't take long for the apartment to become uncomfortably warm and sticky. I also wondered, every time the power went out in the summer, how people managed to live down here before air-conditioning. I know the houses here were built to be cooler on the inside, but there's only so much a breeze can do in July.

I guess they were used to it back then. Ugh.

Life expectancy wasn't very high then, either.

My eyes adjusted to the gloom. It was still cool inside, but with five of us up here it wouldn't stay that way for very long. I opened the junk drawer and got out the long lighter for the hurricane candles. I lit the three lined up alongside the sink, and their glow brightened the room some. Colin and Frank did the same to the blasphemy candles on the coffee table. I walked across the room and opened the curtains to let in some more gloomy light. The windows were rattling in their frames, and I could see the palm trees on that side of the building snapping back and forth in wind gusts. Water was hitting the window so fast I couldn't see much else.

I was very glad to be inside.

We'd done all our hurricane prep work on the house last night, of course, after I got back from hitting every store I could, trying to get everything we needed. I managed to find the last case of water in the CVS on Prytania Street—experience taught me the last place to check was drugstores. We'd put everything in the refrigerator and the freezer inside garbage bags, a trick we learned after Katrina; if everything was spoiled, you could just remove the bags much easier than taking out rotting meat (chicken will eventually liquefy, as I learned to my horror). The shutters on the first-floor windows were closed and latched. I'd closed the curtains before going to bed because who needed to see outside during a hurricane?

The liquor bottles were lined up on the counter at the far end, by the microwave and toaster, should we decide to take the edge off with liquor. There was an ounce of the best Thai weed Mom and Dad had gotten in years stashed in my cigar box under the living room table.

And we could always move up to the main house once the storm passed and indulge in their generator.

These windows were supposed to resist wind gusts from a Category 5 hurricane, or so Papa Diderot claimed over dinner last night. Seeing how far those palm trees were bending made my stomach a bit queasy. I wished the windows on the second floor had shutters like the ones on the first floor…but the first-floor windows were at much higher risk from flying debris than we were up here on the second floor.

Or so I hoped.

Was it my imagination, or was it already getting sticky in here?

"I still have bars," Colin said, frowning at his phone,

his face glowing blue from the screen, "and I seem to have a Wi-Fi signal." He tapped at his screen. "Yeah, my phone switched over to the Wi-Fi from the main house. Pretty strong signal." He laughed, like he always does when he sees what Papa Diderot named the main house network: NOT_FBI_SURVEILLANCE.

Frank gave him the idea and Papa laughed for about five minutes...before making the change.

Frank fits in almost eerily well with my family.

"Are they on the generator at the main house?" Frank asked. "Or do they still have their power?"

"Let me look." I crossed the gloomy room to the other side. Since the one end of the room was the kitchen, there were no windows on that wall. I pulled back the curtains, wiped fog off one of the lower panes, and pressed my face against the glass. It was darker on this side of the building, and there were a lot of trees in the big yard. I could make out the dark shape of the house. I squinted, but yes, I could see there were no lights on the higher floor but a dim one coming from the study windows where they'd set up Aunt Erica. "I just see some dim light on the first floor," I called back, "so yeah, the generator's working." I started to turn back away from the window, but something caught my eye in the direction of the dower house. But when I squinted and stared, I didn't see anything. Must have just been a trick of the rain, I decided, turning away as the wind picked up again.

I closed my eyes. This was a big gust, the kind that whistled and howled like it was trying to talk to us, telling us that it didn't matter how strong the house was built, there was no shelter strong enough to withstand the force of angry tropical wind looking to prove nothing human could survive against the force of nature. I took deep breaths as the wind battered the building, trying not to think it was trying to get underneath it and tip the whole structure over onto its side.

The wind's prying fingers crept along the house, hugging and stroking the walls, trying to find cracks or holes, anything to get inside. The branches of the massive live oak outside brushed against the walls, adding the horrible sound of scratching to the hellish symphony being conducted outside.

The music of the storm got louder as the wind sped up again, and involuntarily I tried to dig my toes into the floor through my sandals and brace myself, like the muscles in my legs could somehow keep the building anchored against the rising fury from the Gulf. A shutter somewhere downstairs worked loose in the wind and began slamming against the side of the building like a bass drum trying to set a dance beat. My teeth started chattering, and I hugged myself, rubbing my hands on my cold arms. No one spoke, and I looked around in the grayish gloom. Everyone grimaced as the wind continued building. I knew my body was reacting to my subconscious, reacting to past storms and dredging up the old fear. Did I take my anxiety pill? I hated riding out hurricanes, always had. There's always that fear of the unknown, and smaller storms could be more destructive than bigger ones. I wished we hadn't lost power and could still get updates from The Weather Channel.

There was a cracking sound from somewhere inside, and the thought *The wind is going to pick us up and send us to Oz* raced through my head. I felt hysterical laughter begin rising up inside me because I flashed from the movie to the street corner in front of Oz on Bourbon Street.

Just when it seemed like the wind might never stop, the gust ended. Before we could catch our breath, even more rain started deluging down from the sky.

And this was an outer band. The *real* storm wasn't even close yet.

The loose shutter banged against the side of the house again.

I picked up one of the hurricane lamps, struck a long match, and lit the wick, putting the flute back over it. Light filled the room. "I'm going to go fix that shutter before it drives me crazy," I said.

"I'll go down with you and check on the Lab guys," Venus said.

Holding the lantern high, I led her down the back stairs. When we reached the bottom, I opened the door to the garage on the left as she started opening her umbrella to go out to the street.

I held up the lamp as I walked into the garage. Unlike upstairs, this was a big open room. At one point, this had been where the carriages were kept, before it housed a limousine that was also long gone now. I vaguely remembered it from when I was a child. The chauffeur's name was Martin, and he had coppery red hair and freckles across his face and always a smile for the grandson of his employer. I think he retired, and Papa and Maman decided they didn't need a personal driver or to keep up a limousine anymore.

The room was filled with piles of boxes and loose furniture under muslin tarps, yellowing with age and covered in dust. Cobwebs dangled from the ceiling, and there was a solitary ceiling fan/chandelier in the direct center. We'd never been allowed in here when we were kids visiting, and I'd never given the building much of a thought. It was just a stucco building in the far corner of the grounds, right on the sidewalk on Chestnut Street. Kind of like the dower house, another building on the grounds, usually vacant. Visitors always stayed at the main house.

Twice now, I thought as I picked my way through the dusty obstacle course, *I've thought I've seen something at the dower house out of the corner of my eye. It's probably just my imagination, right?*

Yeah, that was all it was. I didn't sense anything, so it wasn't anything supernatural, the Goddess sending me a warning or some ghost trying to communicate with me. Yeah, that only happened once, but once was enough, thank you very much.

But it wouldn't hurt to try to read the cards again once Blaine and Venus were on their way.

I sighed as the shutter banged again. It was the one in the far back corner, the exact opposite of where the stairs were, of course. I kept looking down in case there were any rodents or their friends sheltering from the storm as I stepped around a covered chair and nearly bumped into another stack of file boxes, cryptic messages written on their faces with black Magic Marker. The air was thicker down here, too. The stifling closeness of the air going stale upstairs was much worse down here. I could feel sweat drops forming along my scalp and the back of my neck.

Blam! Blam! Blam!

I set the lantern down on a workbench a decent distance from the window, so the wind wouldn't knock it over. The last thing I needed was an oil fire down here with all this old paper and furniture. The fire department wouldn't be able to come for quite a while.

I braced myself, unlocked the window, and pushed it up.

The wind was blowing from the direction of the street, so it didn't blow any water in right away, but I was hit in the face with the sticky damp heat. The wind took the shutter again and slammed it against the side of the house, with a loud bang I felt in my fillings, and held it there so it couldn't swing back. The other shutter was held in place by a long black metal rod and wasn't moving. It was the shutter with the latch on it, so somehow the insert had worked its way loose.

And the black metal rod that should be holding the free shutter in place, matching the other one, was on the floor.

Which…wasn't dusty.

Weird.

I picked up the lantern and swept it around, checking the floor.

The pathway I'd taken through the obstacle course was dust-free, but the floor was still covered in dust everywhere else.

So someone had to have swept up the dust.

Maybe because they didn't want their footprints to show?

I shivered. The thought that someone had been in here without us knowing wasn't pleasant.

I walked back to the window. There was some superglue resting on the workbench. I opened it and squeezed the bottle. A small bubble appeared at the end that sucked back inside once I stopped squeezing. If the rod that held the shutter closed needed to be glued back on, I was set.

I was going to have to stick my head out there.

Maybe it wouldn't be so bad. No rain was blowing in, after all.

I took a deep breath and took the plunge.

And was instantly sorry.

It was like sticking my head under a running showerhead. The individual drops were hitting me so fast and hard my scalp and neck were stinging. I reached over, the rainwater running into my eyes and down my neck. I grabbed the bottom of the shutter, but it was slick and wet and slipped out of my hands. I pulled my head back in out of the storm and wiped my face dry with my tank top. Water was running down my back and dripping from the back of my shirt, getting my butt wet, too. I plunged my head back out into the downpour and reached for the shutter again, this time sticking my fingers through the lowest slats to make sure I had a good grip. I pulled it shut.

But after latching it shut, I realized that the latch was secure. And the slots for the rod to hold it closed were intact. No loose screws anywhere.

Someone unlatched the shutter and took the rod off. Someone had swept up the dust on the floor to hide footprints.

Someone had been inside the house. They'd opened this window for some reason.

I jiggled the latch, wondering why the shutter hadn't been slamming against the house all night.

Yet another mystery to solve on this hurricane morning.

I picked up the lantern and walked back to the door to the back stairs, examining the floor this time. The floor had been swept clean all the way to the door. Standing there, looking back into the gloomy darkness, at the piles of boxes and sheet-covered forms—yes, the way I'd gone was the most direct route to that window. So whoever had been inside had gone from the back stairs to the window.

Had they come in through the back door?

I hated that we didn't have a burglar alarm on the house. There were security cameras—

The security cameras.

Maman and Papa Diderot had gotten security cameras set up all over the property, including on the sidewalks, four or five years ago. I'd forgotten and really wasn't happy with myself as I started climbing the back steps. We could have checked the footage from the cameras—the video was fed live to a security firm, where the images were monitored—but with the power out, were they still working? I burst into the upstairs, excited to tell them we might have the killer on film, whether committing the crime or dumping the body. I grabbed a towel from the bathroom on the way to the living room to wipe myself down. "Venus and Blaine aren't back?"

"No," Frank replied. "I'm thinking we should probably—when we can—move on over to the main house. The streets are starting to flood, and if we get water on the first level, we'll have trouble getting out later, and"—he winced before continuing—"we have a couple of leaks. We put out buckets and towels, but I don't trust the roof."

The carriage house roof had been damaged by Katrina. The insurance adjustors theorized a tornado caused by the hurricane had ripped off the roof, spreading its debris and tiles and splintered pieces of wood all over the yard. With everything in the city needing repair, pretty much, Papa Diderot hadn't been able to get anyone to come in and replace the roof for almost a year, a fluttering, weighted blue tarp standing in for a solid roof that entire time. They'd ended up having to gut the entire second floor and rebuild it, which was why it now had an open-floor plan instead of being broken up into proper rooms. It was never going to be rented out and was just an extra place on the property for a couch-surfing relative to use, or for visiting guests if the dower house was occupied.

Also, there had been a lot of shoddy construction done around the city in the wake of Katrina and the flood.

But the new roof *had* survived every storm since.

Probably not a tornado. Probably termites, meaning the place needed tenting.

Even better.

"Colin thinks so, too," Frank went on. "Plus, the longer the power's out, the warmer it's going to get in here."

I tossed the towel and my tank top into the sink. It did feel muggy and stuffy. I could feel sweat starting to form in my armpits and on my scalp. I'd been more wet than Aquaman for most of the morning, and now dashing across the soggy lawn yet again was on the agenda?

Would I ever feel dry again?

"We'll have to wait for this band to pass," I replied. I could feel the postnasal drip forming in my sinuses. Yeah, it was getting muggier. Frank was messing with his phone.

"I'm waiting for the radar map to load." Frank stared at his phone like I hadn't said anything. "It's taking forever. Come on come on come on," he muttered.

"We'll make a run for it the minute the rain stops again,"

I said. It had been bad enough getting over there earlier—the yard was probably even wetter and had more debris in it by now.

At least you don't have to go out in it to do your job, I reminded myself, thinking about Venus, Blaine, and the other cops.

"It looks like this current band is passing, and yes, the bitch has gone back offshore. She's just sitting there, in the Gulf." Frank frowned. "What other storm did you say did this?"

"Isaac, in 2012." We get so many it's sometimes hard to keep track. At least that storm had blocked the late August sun and the storm conditions had made it cooler. It took about two days for the apartment to get unbearable, and we fled uptown to the generator in the Diderot House. We'd been able to get back to the apartment on Friday, when all the queens started arriving for Decadence. The sun came back out for Decadence and didn't leave her sister, the humidity, behind. By late Friday, the Quarter was filled with wasted, barely clothed queens, and you'd never guess we'd had a hurricane earlier in the week.

This year, my birthday was only a week away, so Decadence (which we count as our anniversary) wasn't for another three weeks, so Hester wouldn't affect it at all.

Well, so long as Hester's storm surge didn't break through the levees.

I followed Frank back over to the living area, carrying my lamp. Colin was fiddling with his phone. I heard a door shut so walked back over to the front stairs and looked down. The door to the steps was open, and Venus and Blaine were huddled inside, dripping wet. "How are they doing?" I called out, walking down to meet them.

"Taking the body to the morgue," Venus replied. "They just took off."

"They should have waited for the rain to stop," I said, stepping past them and opening the outside door a crack. Chestnut Street was under about an inch of water, and the storm drains were filled with rushing, swirling water littered with leaves.

"Streets are flooding, and it's just going to get worse," Blaine replied. "Better to get moving before things get too bad."

"Well, if you're going to be staying here for long, you're going to need to move your SUV into the driveway at the main house before the water gets higher," I pointed out. "Or would you rather come back to interview everyone at the main house?"

They exchanged a glance, seeming to communicate without speaking, and Venus replied, "Well, we might as well ride out the storm here as anywhere," she said slowly. "At least we'll be working."

"We're going over to the main house, too," I said. "We're going across the lawn."

"I'll move the car," Blaine said, removing the key clip on his belt. "Scotty, wouldn't it be easier for all of us to ride over there, rather than running across the lawn during a hurricane?"

I wasn't in the mood to get soaked another time. "Thanks, Blaine, that's a good idea." I thought for a moment. My car and Taylor's were in the driveway, along with Maman and Papa Diderot's cars. "Let me run up and get the guys."

I dashed back up the stairs and explained to Frank and Colin what was going on. They grabbed their phones and umbrellas and followed me back down the stairs.

Blaine opened the door, and the wind tried to rip it out of his hands. The wind was picking up again, and it blew the heavy rain directly at us as we all followed Blaine out the door. I put my left hand over my eyes to try to keep the rain out, but it was futile. I splashed through the water and grabbed the back door handle. Once I started to pull it open, the wind grabbed it and tried tearing it off the SUV. I jumped into the back seat, and Frank followed as I scooted across to the other side. Venus was fighting to close the front passenger door behind her, and finally, we were all inside with the doors shut, catching our breath and not speaking.

We sat there in the SUV for a moment, the rain striking a steady beat on the roof. I looked out my window. I couldn't see anything. Maybe taking the SUV, even if it was just around the corner and up the driveway, wasn't such a good idea after all.

But it wouldn't be much safer to run across the yard, would it?

"The band should be past soon," Colin said, looking down at his phone. "We should be ready to make a break for it as soon as the rain stops." Blaine shifted the car into reverse and backed off the sidewalk. I was just about to say *Don't forget the gutters* just as he shifted into drive. There was a loud crunching noise, and the front right side of the SUV sank about a foot. Frank and Colin slid across the seat into me.

"*Fuck.*" Blaine slapped the gearshift. He put the car into reverse, but it didn't go anywhere, the back tires spinning and burning rubber on the pavement. He put it back into drive again, with no luck. He turned the keys off and banged his forehead on the steering wheel.

"You'll need a tow truck to get out of this," Venus observed coolly. "Guess we're stuck here till the storm passes."

"Looks like we'll have to go across the lawn after all," I said as Frank and Colin peeled themselves off me. I opened the door and stepped out, splashing through the standing water over to the side gate. I quickly unlocked it and pushed it open. Water that had pooled behind it washed over my already soaking feet. The wind was still blowing, but not as strong as it had been. The rain did seem to be lessening a bit.

This was as good a time as any to make a run to the main house.

I tried closing the gate after Blaine went through, pointlessly clicking his key fob to lock his vehicle. The gate was heavy, which was why no one ever used it, but the flow of rushing water down the sloping lawn made it even harder to close. Blaine helped me, and we were both completely soaked by the time the lock clicked shut.

There were tree branches in all sizes and shapes scattered across the wet grass like abandoned toys, and I could also see some roofing tiles. If tiles had come off the roof of the carriage house…But they could have come from anywhere, carried by the whims of the wind and finding their final resting place on our lawn. And the lawn was soggy. Since the lawn sloped from the main house to the street in pretty much every direction, the water was running down the hill much faster than it had been the last time I went up to the house.

The stream of water was a current now, racing rapidly to the lower level of the street. Water was swirling over the flagstones alongside the carriage house, rising a fraction of an inch faster than I wanted to see. The carriage house might take on some water, it looked like, and I was glad we were leaving.

And like switching off a light, the wind and the rain stopped. An eerie calm dropped over the neighborhood. "Follow me," I said and stepped off the flagstones onto the grass. My feet sank into the soggy ground with an audible slurp. I was able to pull my feet up out of it—there was so much water the mud was almost fluid. I took a deep breath and started walking faster, as fast as I could in the inch or so of water above the mushy ground. I took a deep breath and kept going. It was more work than it looked, but walking in water is always a pain in the ass. My legs were getting tired, another reminder I'd not been as faithful about going to the gym as I usually was. I could hear the others splashing along behind me, so I gritted my teeth and kept moving.

After what seemed like an eternity, I finally reached the back gallery stairs yet again. I paused for breath, pretending like I was waiting for everyone else to get there. They were all walking with their heads down, keeping an eye on where they were stepping so they didn't step on a branch or some other errant debris. First Frank, then Colin, and finally Venus reached me. The back door was open, and water shimmered on the gallery in the glow from the flickering gaslight mounted on the back wall.

"The stairs and the gallery are going to be slippery," I warned, raising my voice as the wind began to pick up again. A light sprinkle of rain was starting, too, the drops making rings in the standing water in puddles and pools around the back of the house. The dower house sat behind, all dark and haunted looking. There's a family legend that it's haunted—a long-ago matron moved back there from the main house so her son's wife could take her place, and she slowly pined away, listening to the noise and the music from the parties her son's wife threw, until finally one morning her servant found her in a chair by the big window by the front door. Supposedly, on nights when there's a party at the main house, you could see her form in the window and hear her sad, lonely sighs. Storm and Rain, always the most wretched elder siblings ever, loved scaring me about her ghost, to the point where I wouldn't go near the place for years.

Looking at it again now, I could feel my skin crawling and the hairs on the back of my neck standing up.

I started up the stairs holding the railing and still almost slipped, my wet muddy feet sliding in the water puddled on the stairs. "Hold on to the railing," I called back over my shoulder.

"Scotty?"

Nora was standing in the doorway, wiping her hands on an apron. I winked at her and climbed up onto the gallery. Frank and Colin soon joined me.

Venus started up the stairs gingerly. She was wearing what would have been sensible heels under normal conditions. She seemed unsteady. Her foot slipped on the second step, but she caught herself. More confident, she started moving faster, but when she put her right foot on the top step, the sky opened, and water just poured down onto her. Startled, she lost her balance and went over backward.

It seemed to happen in slow motion.

One moment she was putting her foot up, the next she was falling backward. I reached for her, trying to grab her shirt, but my fingertips just brushed against it. Down she went, landing on her ass on a lower step before bouncing off and hitting the ground with her left leg under her at an angle so bad I cringed. She screamed, loud enough to hear over the rain.

I went down the steps as fast as I safely could. "Are you okay?" I shouted over the rain.

She was sitting up, water splashing all over both our bodies. "I think I broke my ankle, Scotty," Venus said, through gritted teeth. "Help me."

CHAPTER SEVEN

TEN OF CUPS, REVERSED

Chance of betrayal

It often surprises people that I'm very good in a crisis.

I'll be the first to admit that my early life as a profligate single gay man in the Quarter didn't exactly lend itself to being taken seriously, nor did flunking out of college after two years. Everyone thought I was flighty and silly and would never settle down. I don't think I've settled down much since meeting the boys, but since Frank—a serious older man who worked for the FBI for twenty years—moved in, that's started to change. I still get underestimated, but the first time I found a dead body I had to learn how to be good in a crisis fast.

And the first rule of being good in a crisis is to stay calm.

Sure, we were between bands of a hurricane, I'd found a dead body, and now Venus had broken her ankle, but it's a challenge to overcome, not something to freak out about.

Freaking out never did anyone any good.

Venus's ankle looked horrible, though.

What a fucking day this was turning into. A dead body, a hurricane, and now Venus had broken her ankle.

At least the rain was letting up.

She was sitting upright on the grass, calmly getting soaked. Her legs were stretched out in front of her, and she was sitting in about an inch of muddy water. Her ankle was continuing to swell, and the skin around it was turning an ugly dark shade of bruise purple. The deluge had lessened to a light sprinkle, but the thick gray clouds overhead were picking up speed again—which meant another storm band would be here soon.

"We need to get her inside, and fast," I shouted, kneeling beside her. "You okay, Venus?"

Venus's face was taut, but she managed to choke out, during a grimace of pain, "Doing great. Never better."

"I'm sure we've got painkillers at the main house—Erica can spare a couple," I said as Colin splashed over to us. I was about to tell her to put an arm around my shoulders so we could lift her, but before I could get the words out, Colin squatted down and slipped an arm under her hips. She put her arm around his shoulders. He literally just straightened his legs and rose, with her securely in his arms.

"Got her," Colin said, not even straining. I always forgot he's ridiculously strong. "Can you get the door for me?"

Venus gave me a surprised look at the ease he'd lifted her with. Her eyes closed, and her teeth clenched as he took a tentative first step. Colin splashed his way over to the flagstone path and started carrying her back up the steps. Frank, Blaine, and I walked ahead of them. I opened the back door for them and stuck my head inside. The kitchen was empty. I turned back to the gallery as Colin carried Venus up to the gallery.

The sky lit up white and stank of ozone. The hair on my arms stood up, and we were almost immediately deafened by a clap of thunder and a cracking sound. The lightning bolt had hit one of the big live oaks along the fence along the back end of the property, on the far end of the dower house. The branch flipped, did a one-eighty, the flames sizzling out when they hit the standing water on the lawn.

"Christ," Blaine breathed out as the wind started picking up again.

"Everyone inside, now!" I ordered. My legs were aching. Walking through running water over a soupy mud was brutal on my quads. I was about to follow them when I saw a brief flash of light out of the corner of my eye in one of the dower house's windows. Up on the second floor.

I turned my head quickly to look again, but nothing was there now.

If it had been there in the first place.

Just another one of the family ghosts, I figured as I closed the door behind me.

Frank handed me a towel to stand on and another to dry off with. I ran the soft, fluffy white towel down my legs, over my arms and head. I felt better, even with my clothes plastered to my body.

"Nora set out some clothes for us," he said over his shoulder as he walked over to the laundry room. He stood in the doorway, dropped his shorts and underwear, and pulled his tank top over his head. He looked back over at me with a come-hither look.

What could I do? I came hither.

I shut the laundry room door behind me and pulled off my wet clothes. We threw our clothes in the dryer and turned it on. As it started, I dried myself more with the towel before drying Frank's wide, muscular back. I couldn't resist the urge, so I planted a kiss in between his shoulder blades.

He pulled on a pair of black boxers and turned around, kissing me on the forehead. "Tempting as it is to ravish you in here, Nora will be back at any moment." He winked. "And I don't know how she'd take it."

"She seems cool, but why risk her quitting?" I laughed as I pulled a ratty old sea-blue Tulane Green Wave sweatshirt over my head. "I'd hate to do that to Maman. Good help is very hard to find these days." I wiggled my eyebrows at him.

Frank wiped his damp chest hair with the towel. Just looking at him drying himself with a towel, I was reminded how lucky I was. Frank was now in his late fifties but could still pass for being in his forties—early forties, at that. His age always staggered me when I thought about it. He still turned heads whenever we went down to the Fruit Loop to get our gay on in the clubs. Guys were always hitting on him when we danced, or even just stood around sipping our beers. He was a Hot Daddy when I first met him, and an even hotter Daddy now.

And the sex was still incredible. Have I mentioned that already?

We kissed one more time before breaking apart and heading back into the kitchen. "Where's Venus?" I asked, looking out the gallery windows. Like most old homes in New Orleans, all the windows on the first floor were enormous, running upward at least eight feet from the floor. The shutters hadn't been bolted on this side, which was always protected from the wind by the angle of the house. I could see the dower house out there, but the rain was so thick everything seemed distorted. I peered through the gloom and the pouring rain, wondering if I'd see the light again.

It was your imagination, Scotty. No one's over there. Aunt Erica is here, and her nurse is in the morgue.

But I couldn't shake the feeling I was missing something important.

I *hated* that feeling.

"They're getting her all set up in Maman's study," Frank replied, pouring more coffee into his own cup. We both were wearing green sweatpants that were too big in the waist. I retied the strings in mine, tighter, hoping they'd stay up. "Nora gave her one of Erica's oxy–something or another to help with the pain. Blaine thinks she should go to the emergency room, but she thinks they should wait until after the storm passes." He gave me a crooked grin. "He'd have to borrow a car to take her, anyway. His SUV ain't going nowhere anytime soon."

"Touro is pretty close." It was about ten short blocks, if that. It was just on the other side of Louisiana Avenue, up on Prytania. "And if she's on pain pills, she can hardly interrogate anyone." I'd been given oxycodone once, for an abscessed tooth, and could remember nothing of the rest of that day other than enjoying myself tremendously.

I could see why it was so addictive.

"Colin set her ankle and bound it up," Frank went on. "I don't think I want to know much about his medical training, do I?"

There was a lot we didn't know about Colin's former job.

There was a lot I didn't want to know about his former job.

"Well, on a mission it wasn't likely they'd be able to go to hospitals or find a doctor—they'd have to deal with it, right?" I finished my coffee and set the cup in the sink. I was already overcaffeinated, and my nerves were already jangling. The last thing I needed was more. "I bet he can treat wounds and set bones and has a lot of skills we don't even know about." We did know he was a whiz with computers and motors. He often worked on the family cars whenever anyone was having engine trouble. He always said he liked doing it, whenever I worried we took advantage—my sister Rain was notorious for having him check out her car for even the slightest thing she thought wasn't normal—and that he loved working with his hands.

Both Frank and I could attest to just how good Colin was with his hands.

Have I mentioned how incredible the sex is yet? Because it needs to be said, often.

"And if she's on pain meds, she's not going to be doing a whole lot until later, anyway," I replied as my sort of nephew Taylor walked into the kitchen, yawning. He hadn't brushed his hair, which was sticking up in every direction, and there was stubble on his face. "Morning, Taylor." I hoped he wasn't mad at me still.

Taylor had started dating a guy we met through our last

case. Brody. Brody was starting school at Tulane when the semester opened to major in dance, with a ballet specialization. He'd gone to NOCCA, and we'd seen the NOCCA production of *Romeo and Juliet*, in which he played Mercutio and stole the entire ballet right out from under the leads. He had an incredible stage presence, so you couldn't really stop watching him, and he added acting to his dancing more than his castmates. Mercutio was a good role to showcase how great he was onstage.

You didn't get a scholarship to Tulane for dance without being great.

Taylor had wanted Brody to ride out the storm with us, instead of in the shotgun house where he lived with his mother. I'd said no, and the boys backed me in the face of Taylor's angry disappointment. My grandparents were cool about the gay thing, but asking them to let Taylor's eighteen-year-old boyfriend (Taylor had turned twenty-one a few months and multiple murders ago) come stay in their house seemed too much to ask. Frank was the one who pointed out that if anything happened to Brody in the house, Maman and Papa could be liable for it. So we told Taylor no, and he wasn't happy about it.

Taylor rolled his eyes so hard I almost heard them. "Morning," he said, grabbing a mug and filling it.

"You're not still mad at me?"

He made a face. "If this hurricane kills us all, I'd rather not die mad."

"We're not going to die," I replied, shivering. "Don't even say it as a joke, it's bad juju…Have you talked to Brody this morning? I would imagine the circuits are pretty tied up in southeast Louisiana."

"I tried when I got up," he said glumly. "Didn't go through, and then the power went out." He rolled his eyes again, and he got that mutinous look on his face. "If the levees break like during Katrina—"

"*Stop*," Frank roared, coming up behind him and clapping his hand over Taylor's mouth. "Don't say it, and don't even think it."

I'd never bothered warning Taylor about Frank's hurricane phobia. Katrina hadn't been a great experience, but we'd managed to evacuate before the storm arrived. I'd been blasé about the whole thing, thinking that it would miss the city and turn at the last minute, as so many others before had. I didn't think we needed to leave. I never had before. But Frank was nervous, so I'd humored him. I drove us up to north Louisiana to a ranch Papa Diderot owned near Natchitoches. The whole drive up there I kept thinking—and saying—we were wasting our time, while Frank had that grim look on his face.

He had the decency not to say *I told you so* when the levees failed.

We watched all the horror unroll on live television, unable to reach anyone in the family, wondering if our house was still there, smoking joint after joint trying to not freak out. I didn't think the Quarter had flooded, but there was so much chaos and so many conflicting reports. Slowly but surely the rest of the family began showing up at the ranch, filling us in on what it was like, how hard it had been to get out, all of us glued to the television as we watched the horror. We stayed up there until the city reopened, and we found that other than some damage to our balcony, the apartment and the house had withstood the storm well. Neither Frank nor I rode out a storm unless we had to.

Taylor, slippery as a snake, managed to escape from his uncle's arms.

Since Taylor had been drugged and assaulted last Christmas, it's taken him a while to get used to not flinching or reacting to being touched by people unexpectedly. Being with Brody, I thought, was helping him get past it.

The look on his face was troubled. Being grabbed had triggered him.

"Are you hungry?" I said quickly, giving Frank a look.

Taylor just scowled at us both. "Stop acting like I'll break," he snarled. "I'm going back to my room." He clomped heavily across the kitchen and opened the door to the back staircase. The sounds of his heavy footsteps eventually died away. Usually light as a cat, he was stomping to make a point.

Frank sighed. "Sorry, I wasn't thinking." He rubbed his eyes and looked tired.

And I could hear the rain coming down harder and the wind whistling like it was looking for a way to get in...I shivered. *Stop that*, I commanded myself. *That's not helping at all.*

Before I could say anything to make him feel better, my grandmother joined us in the kitchen.

I couldn't help but grin. I loved my grandmother, mainly because she was just too cool for words for a high society Garden District matron who was a powerhouse in the charity fundraiser/ladies-who-lunch set here. In some ways, Maman was a throwback to a distant past, when a lady wore a hat and gloves to have tea or play whist in a drawing room, would never think of leaving the house without a hat or gloves, and never went out in public unless she was completely put together from the top of her head to the heels on her sensible pumps. She always looked calm, cool, and collected. She had a soft, low voice because ladies never raised theirs, you know. But that gentle, ladylike exterior fooled everyone. No one could tell that beneath the manners and the gentleness, she was made of steel and you did *not* want to get on her bad side.

This morning, despite a hurricane coming and a dead body being found, she looked completely unflappable. Her hair was perfectly coiffed, every hair in its place, and she was wearing her green framed glasses that matched the green Tulane sweatshirt she had on, but her pearls were at her neck, and she had, as she would say, her face on. She was wearing black ballet flats like she always did when she was home, and she looked around the room, confused. "I could have sworn I heard Taylor," she said, knitting her brows together over her clear blue eyes. She looked a lot younger than she was, like everyone in the family. Sometimes it was hard for me to grasp that my grandparents were now in their early nineties. They hadn't slowed down much. Maybe they walked a little slower, and maybe their memories weren't as sharp as they used to be, but they were still forces of nature that Storm swore would outlive us all.

I assumed the sweats I was wearing were Storm's, like the ones I'd put on before. They were too big for me, with the pants threatening to slide down at any moment, despite how tightly I'd tied the drawstring. "He went upstairs," I replied.

"I don't know why he didn't invite that friend of his to come ride out the storm with us," she said as she took a bottle of champagne—Dom Pérignon, at that—and twisted at the cork until it popped off easily into her hand with some champagne steam slipping out of the open neck. She filled a glass halfway and finished filling it with orange juice.

Getting older hadn't slowed their drinking down, either.

Oops. Frank and I exchanged a glance, and I wondered how I could get her to not say anything to Taylor about it. I'd *never* hear the end of it if he found out.

I'd hear about it every time I told him no.

To be fair, it's what I would do. I still gave Storm and Rain grief about things they'd done or said to me when we were kids.

Maman smiled at me, reaching for one of her little yellow legal notepads. She was a list maker. "We've got Detective Casanova in my study," she said, writing something on the pad. "What terrible timing for an injury. Colin is fixing her up with a splint—that young man! I swear, there's nothing he can't do!"

Well, you pick up all kinds of mad skills when you're an international espionage agent for decades, I thought. Mom and Dad knew, but we'd kept it from the rest of the family.

It's a lot to explain.

"And Erica is in Papa's study, you three boys are up here now, too," Maman went on, refilling her coffee mug. "Your uncle Misha is here, but he's not come down yet." She wrinkled her brow. "I imagine, though, once it starts getting warmer up there, he'll come down pretty quickly." She hummed and flipped the page and started writing on another. "We can cook out after the hurricane passes—we can bake potatoes on the grill, too—and I think I have those ribs…" Still talking to herself, she took her notepad into the pantry with her.

Having a generator didn't mean the entire house had power. Even Papa Diderot had his limits when it came to spending money, and the power would be out so long that having a generator with its own natural gas line would cost a small fortune. He even groused about how expensive it was to keep the first floor powered. The air conditioning was set to seventy-nine to not draw power from the freezers and the refrigerators. The oven was on the same gas line as the generator, so we could cook. We just couldn't wash clothes or use the microwave or any of the other kitchen gadgets (and Maman had every kitchen gadget imaginable).

My uncle Misha Saltikov was Mom's younger half brother, way closer in age to me than he was to Mom. A long time ago, Papa Diderot had an affair with a Russian ballerina. Unbeknownst to him or the family, Papa had gotten the ballerina pregnant. When she was dying, some thirty or so years later, she wrote my grandmother and told her the truth—that Papa had a son in Russia. He had come over to the United States, had married Maman's best friend Sylvia Overton (it's a long story), but she died a few years ago. Breast cancer, the poor thing. Misha had been devoted to her and was holding her hand when she passed away.

Misha had trained to be an Olympic wrestler since childhood, moving from that into bodybuilding. His biceps were bigger than my head. His heavy Russian accent had faded away over the years until it was hardly noticeable anymore, unless he was excited or upset about something. He fit into the family like he'd been a missing piece of the puzzle we hadn't known we'd needed. He still lived over on Upperline and just bought a gym on Magazine Street, Bodytech.

Not having grown up with the kind of weather we got in southeastern Louisiana, Katrina had traumatized him. Sylvia was an evacuator—Maman used to say if she felt a drop of rain and a strong wind, Sylvia would start packing the car—so they'd been gone when the levees broke after Katrina. Ever since Sylvia passed, he'd taken to coming over to the Diderot House every time a storm threatened. He felt safer being with family. Maman treated him like she treated all of us—like servants that she loved very much, and Maman was known for always being good to her staff. When Mom was young, the house had been staffed by a team; now cleaners came in and did the house from top to bottom every Monday and Thursday, and only Nora lived in. Mom hated having that many servants around, and gradually Papa and Maman had come around and started doing things themselves. Maman herself was a great cook, but it wasn't something she did very often. Whenever she did, I wondered how Mom had learned nothing from her mother.

Growing up with my parents with their love of all things tofu had been challenging.

It already felt muggy in the kitchen, and I could feel sweat starting to form on my scalp. There was another crash of thunder, and the wind picked up again. This gust, shrieking and howling and whistling as it tried to find its way inside—or to pick the house up off its foundations—seemed to last forever, and when it finally died down, even more rain started coming down, so thick and hard, and now I could barely even see the dower house…

I blinked a few times. Wait—what was *that*?

Had I imagined seeing another light over there just now?

You're seeing things because you're thinking about them, I reminded myself. *Who could be over there now? In this weather? Aunt Erica is in Papa's study, and Nurse Pitre, well, she's on her way to the city morgue.*

Maman, still talking to herself, walked back out of the pantry, dropped her pad on the island, and carried her coffee out of the kitchen.

I walked back over to the back door. Frank watched me warily while leaning against the counter. I opened the heavy oak door, and the howling wind got louder. Between the wind and the steady downpour, it was like I could almost see the gusts moving the water through the grayness. I could see more clearly with the door open, but it was so gloomy and the rain—

"What are you doing?" Frank came up behind me, putting his hands on my shoulders. "Probably should keep the door closed, don't you think? We don't want the wind—"

"I thought I saw something." I squinted, stared as hard as I could. "But that can't be, can it? I couldn't have seen something in the windows over there?" It had to be my imagination. It's no wonder I was seeing things. I mean, hadn't we already found a dead body this morning?

Yeah, that could only happen to me.

Frank nuzzled the back of my neck. "Isn't the dower house haunted?" he murmured, sliding his hands down my back and then bringing them around to the front. He pulled me into a hug. "I mean, if you can be psychic, it stands to reason that ghosts might be real, too."

I'd communicated with a dead spirit once, and it wasn't something I ever wanted to do again, to be honest. That had been a special case, I figured later, where a restless spirit who'd left something undone had to come back to finally put an end to the problems he'd caused before he died. Every time I'd spoken to the spirit—in my head, he never took a corporeal form—I'd been left feeling like I was running on empty, that my batteries had been depleted, and it took me a while to get over it. The problem with that was I'd been high on adrenaline, trying to save someone's life, so it didn't hit me until it was all over. I think I'd spent a week in bed—with Frank and Colin, so it wasn't just me dawdling around—but yeah, not something I'd want to experience again.

"Maybe I should go over there after this band passes," I said, not really wanting to. The rain was just cascading down in sheets. I could see water gushing out of the gutter spouts. There were gargoyle-headed spouts on some of the gutters on the upper floors. Water was coming down those pipes like a waterfall and drowning the yard. It looked like the water might be rising enough to get inside the dower house. Which would mean Aunt Erica would have to stay up here until repairs could be made.

I hoped nothing happened to the carriage house.

I closed the door. Just my overactive imagination, that's all. My nerves were on edge. My adrenaline had spiked several times, and I was starting to feel tired. And I did have a vivid imagination, right? And all this stress and finding a body and the storm—yeah, it's no wonder that I was seeing things.

No one could be in the dower house because no one (besides us) was stupid enough to go outside in the early stages of a hurricane. "Any more news on the storm?"

Frank sighed. "It looks like it's just sitting off the coast, churning and spinning and picking up more water—and maybe more power—before it comes back ashore. There's a model that shows it heading east along the coast instead, but I think that's wishful thinking. It's going to come back and hit us hard." He turned me around and kissed my forehead. "Grand Isle and Port Fouchon are getting hammered."

Hurricanes were very unkind to Grand Isle, which had shrunk significantly in size as our coastline eroded and the seas rose. The sea was out of our control, but the erosion of the coastline was entirely the fault of corporate greed and corrupt politicians only interested in their own short-term gains, hoping the long-term losses would wait to become a code red after they'd made their bank and either cashed out or died. Port Fouchon was in Plaquemines Parish, and mostly a coastal community. It was where offshore oil workers shipped out to and from the rigs. Most of its economy was supplying the rigs in the Gulf, each one a ticking time bomb. How many potential Deepwater Horizons were out there just waiting to dump millions more barrels of oil into the fragile Gulf ecosystem? New Orleans had smelled like burning oil for months.

"Let's go check on Venus," I said, kissing the base of his throat, "or should I go upstairs and change my clothes first?"

He swatted me lightly on the butt. "Yeah, you don't want to drop trou in front of Venus."

I made a face at him, grabbed my phone and my coffee, and headed down the hallway to the beautiful main circular staircase, the upper landings and floors couched in darkness. I took a deep breath—I've never been a fan of the dark. I switched on my flashlight app and pointed it up to the landing, walking quickly up the hardwood stairs. It was a stunning hanging staircase, and it opened out wide at the bottom, built to accommodate hoop skirts back in the day when young ladies still dressed that way. There had been a ballroom on the first floor, but Papa's father had turned that into other rooms because they'd stopped using the ballroom.

Sometimes I tried to imagine what it must have been like to live here back then, when all the rooms on the fourth floor were taken by live-in servants and there was no air-conditioning, when Diderot men were expected to be Southern gentlemen, and their women were ladies with rules for every last bit of their conduct and appearance. It's easy to romanticize the past like that, but what was it like for the servants? This wasn't the original Diderot house—the original had burned in the late nineteenth century, and this place was built on its ruins, same style and look and colors—that lovely dusky rose the outside was painted, with the beautiful black wrought-iron railings and balconies and galleries—but bigger. The Diderots had always had money but truly flourished around the turn of the century, keeping that legacy of generational wealth going, each succeeding generation building it into more. Our family fortunes hadn't declined because of a wastrel heir or anything, like other old families, although sometimes I wondered if my generation would be the one to go broke.

The second-floor landing had a doorway out to a balcony on the right, one that sat over the beveled windows on the first floor that jutted out several feet beyond the walls of the house. The shutters over the French doors were closed and latched, but rattling and shaking in the wind.

Tempting as it was to go over there and try to see out through the slats, it wasn't a good idea. The second floor was very dark. What little light there was outside was blocked by the shutters, and of course there was no power. Back in the olden days, there used to be gas lamps mounted on the walls. Maybe it wouldn't be such a bad idea to suggest Maman and Papa have the gas lamps remounted—

And then I heard a loud thump from somewhere above me.

CHAPTER EIGHT

PAGE OF SWORDS

Certain types of spying

I aimed my phone and the flashlight app up the stairs.

Of course, I couldn't see anything past the landing. I'd have to go up to see what that was. I hoped I'd discover the source of the thump on the third floor.

I swallowed. I'd never been comfortable in my grandparents' house, but the fourth floor was the worst.

Just staring up into the darkness beyond the light beam, I could feel a pinpoint headache starting between my eyes.

Like every other old house in New Orleans, the Diderot House had lots of history and legends and ghost stories. (The ghost in the dower house stays there.) The original house was built before the Civil War and only had three floors. Before emancipation, the enslaved workers lived up on that top floor. The Diderots had been financially strapped after the war, which was when they sold off some of their land—the original plot was huge. The family fortunes started turning around again after Reconstruction ended. When the original house burned in the 1880s, they had the money to build a bigger, more ornate and opulent house that was one of the showpieces of the Garden District. It still was—even though Maman Diderot refused to allow tours inside.

I'd always seen the house as a symbol of the awful way my family got rich. It's bad enough knowing my ancestors not only enslaved people but had a sugar plantation…which were known for their brutality and horrors. There were also Black Diderots in Orleans Parish—the prewar Diderots apparently also partook in the horror that is remembered as *plaçage*—which sounds so much less abusive than the reality. No one in the family talked about that history much. Mom sometimes talked about tracing the heritage of the Black Diderots but never did anything about it. Storm thought she only brought it up to annoy Papa Diderot.

Maybe I should do it. It was cowardly to never acknowledge the past's reality and to pretend the stories about the family are quirky and charming, rather than truly disturbing. And it could be interesting. The older I got, the more interested in family history I became.

But I wanted to know the whole story, not the dressed-up one that covered up reality to make modern descendants feel better about themselves.

When the house was rebuilt after the fire, the newly built fourth floor was used for the live-in servants. There were stories about the servants, too, only mentioned in whispers and never said aloud. Several maids had disappeared over the years, with a purse full of Diderot money and a womb filled with a Diderot under the bar sinister. Diderot men might have been captains of industry, they might have funded philanthropies and built libraries, but they were typical men of their time: They thought they had a right to women's bodies and indulged whenever they could.

I don't think I've ever felt truly comfortable, or been able to relax, in my grandparents' mansion. Too many things have happened here, too many people have died, too much anger and grief for the past to rest quietly. I think my *gift* has a lot to do with that discomfort. Nothing ever spoke to me here, but there were places in this house where I was always uncomfortable. I got the worst sinus headaches here, and when I was a kid, I thought the house hated me, like it had a mind and a heart and a soul.

How Mom managed to survive growing up in this house was a mystery to me. Papa and Maman said she was always headstrong, even as a child, and had always had strong opinions about right and wrong. She had to be strong to grow up in this house, in this neighborhood, with all the things that went along with being a girl in high New Orleans society. Mom had to do all the things that all proper young ladies of the Garden District did: dancing school, etiquette lessons, high school at McGehee, and she was supposed to also go to the SMU and be a Kappa like all Diderot women did. She wound up in the courts of several krewes but never wanted to be Queen and hated everything about it, including riding on the floats in the Carnival parades. She'd hated every bit of the social swirl of the city, and after she was a Maid of Comus, she told my grandparents flatly she was finished with krewes and balls. To this day she complained about not being able to go out on that Fat Tuesday because that night was the Meeting of the Courts of Comus and Rex, followed by their combined balls.

Maman still shakes her head when she thinks about Mom throwing away her chance to be Queen of Carnival, but Mom was adamant.

Our house in the French Quarter was a lot smaller than the Diderot House, but it was cozier and felt more like home. The Diderot House always seemed like a museum (Mom said mausoleum), and going there for parties and holidays wasn't a lot of fun for me. I've always had a vivid imagination, and a big spooky house in the Garden District with a sordid past and chock full of ghosts (if you believed in that sort of thing, which I did) meant the house often played a role in my nightmares…

And that didn't make me feel warmer about the house.

I found nothing of note on the third floor and returned to the staircase.

I took a step up, and swallowed. *You have to always check out any odd noise during a hurricane*, I reminded myself, *in case it's something you need to do something about.*

I really wanted to run back down to the first floor and let Frank or Colin do it.

Mom always said you can't help the family you're born into, but you can learn from—and how to live with—their crimes. There were all kinds of stories about the house and tragedies that happened in it. The lower floors all had high ceilings, but the top floor's ceiling wasn't quite as high. The house's main roof formed an A shape and branched off into flatter sections. Those flatter sections still had a slight slope to drain rainwater and keep it from pooling. Even so, there were always problems with roof leaks and termites up there.

I've never liked it up there. The air always felt too... *close* up there, and it smelled musty, mildewy, and dusty. The ceiling fans were always on because it got so hot up there in the summer, and the air-conditioning couldn't keep up. When I was little, all I could think about were the servants, living up there in their hot, cramped little rooms. Storm told me once there were several ghosts who roamed the top floor. I'd never sensed any, but that didn't mean anything. Being sort of psychic and not understanding how it worked could be frustrating. Sometimes it worked, sometimes it didn't. I'd communed with a ghost a long time ago, but that was the only time that's happened.

Every house in New Orleans is haunted, but you'd never know if you needed me to sense their presence.

But there shouldn't be anyone up there.

Or anything.

Maybe there was a leak, and the thump I'd heard had something to do with that?

I couldn't just go back downstairs without checking, especially with an imminent hurricane.

The bluish light from my phone's flashlight cast long and creepy shadows.

Well, standing here thinking about it isn't making it any easier, I reminded myself and continued up the stairs toward the fourth-floor landing.

I coughed. The air was thick and cloying. The humidity was much worse up here. My scalp and underarms were starting to get wet, and it was kind of hard to breathe. Nothing to do but keep going—

"Scotty?"

I almost jumped out of my skin. I spun around, almost losing my balance and tumbling back down to the third floor. The light from my phone lit up Taylor, who had a strange look on his face. Confusion and concern? "Sheesh"—I leaned against the carved balustrade, wiping at my damp forehead with the tail of my sweatshirt—"you almost gave me a heart attack!"

"Sorry." Taylor put his hands up to block his eyes from the glare, and I turned it around. "But why are you going up there? Why aren't you downstairs with everyone else?"

I chuckled. "Well, these sweats are Storm's, I think—"

"So they're too big," Taylor finished for me.

"Yes." I smiled at him. "And I keep having to pull them up, and…yeah." Yes, I used to dance in underwear or jocks or thongs in gay bars for tips when I was younger, but my family didn't need to see me in my drawers.

"But why are you going up there?"

"Well, I was going to go see if there's anything that would fit me in the catch-all room." The catch-all room, which was where Nora had retrieved clothes for us from, was just what it was called—a guest bedroom on the fourth floor that no one ever stayed in, so Maman used it to collect things left behind by guests. Maman's mother had died in that room long before I was born, so she didn't like letting people stay in it. It was painted lavender, and her mother's old canopy bed was still in there. The cabinets and armoires were full of hats, coats, shirts, pants, and various other women's items and accessories from almost a century ago. We all left clothes here all the time. "But when I was coming up the stairs, I thought I heard something up here."

"Oh, it was probably just Gabe and Vangie." He waved his hand. "They love it up there on the fourth floor."

I exhaled. Of course. Gabriel and Evangeline, aka Gabe and Vangie, were Maman's five-year-old Maine coons. They were enormous, the size of bobcats, but very sweet and loving and gentle. They were also gorgeous. Gabe was black with white streaks, while Vangie was a tabby with orange and black and white stripes and circles. From the same litter, both had adorable tufts of hairs in their big ears and around their toes. There was a room on the third floor that was just for them—there were all kinds of cat toys and trees and jungle gyms and whatever Maman came across when searching online to spoil them even further. Their litter boxes were also in the room, but their food and water were down in the kitchen. They had cat beds but slept with Maman in her bedroom suite. They each weighed between thirty and forty pounds, so if one jumped down from a height…there would be a thump.

I didn't *need* to go up there and check anything out, did I?

Don't be afraid of the fourth floor—you're an adult now.

The fourth fucking floor.

The only time I can remember going up to the fourth floor when I was a kid was when I was trying to get away from Uncle Luke's bratty twins. Travis and Trevor were Storm's age and assholes for as long as I could remember. That was another reason I disliked the Diderot House. Family holidays meant my uncle and aunt would be driving over from Houston with their wretched kids. They loved picking on me, refused to call me Scotty and only called me Milton, and loved hitting me.

They were both bigger than me, so I had to be careful to not let them catch me alone.

It was the Thanksgiving after my tenth birthday, maybe? I was still small and hadn't started wrestling yet. All through brunch they kept looking across the table at me, whispering to each other, and smirking. They'd started growing and getting bigger already—it seemed like they'd doubled in size since the last time I'd seen them—and I wasn't about to let them corner me or drag me off to some secluded place where no one could hear me screaming for help. I wasn't going to fall for their fake friendly act, designed to get me to go off with them alone so they could pound on me and make me miserable. I often wondered if they could somehow sense I was gay and that was what made them such assholes. Then a holiday would roll around again and I'd remember they were just assholes to begin with. They were awful to their parents and disrespectful to mine. I managed to slip away unseen and climbed the back staircase all the way up to the fourth floor. I was reading a Hardy Boys book in one of the unused bedrooms when I heard them in the hallway, looking for me.

"Come out, Milton, come out and play with us." I could never tell their voices apart. They sounded the same to me. It was eerie how alike they were, sometimes finishing each other's sentences and always operating as one unit, like they didn't have individual identities.

My blood ran cold, and I looked around the room for a place to hide. I debated under the bed or the armoire. It was dirty under the bed, though, and I was still wearing my nice clothes. The armoire it was! I tiptoed across the room, turned the key in its lock, and opened the door. I was relieved to see there were no drawers in the bottom—it was just a big open space for long dresses or coats or something. I stepped inside, pulled the door closed, and waited.

Looking back, my only excuse was that I was still a kid

and hadn't quite figured out the *keep myself safe* thing yet. The overhead light was on, and I'd left the key in the lock.

Sure enough, they were inside the room in a matter of moments.

My heart sank when I heard one of them say, "He's here somewhere—he left his book on the bed."

I cursed at myself.

And then I heard the key turning in the lock.

They locked me in.

I tried to open the door.

It didn't move.

I rattled it, only to hear them laughing at me outside.

I started panicking and started screaming for them to let me out.

When I stopped screaming because my throat was hurting, I couldn't hear them.

I was alone up there on the fourth floor.

Would anyone even think of looking for me up here?

I didn't know how long I was trapped inside that armoire. I did know that I fell asleep, and the twins got into a lot of trouble, which made them want to punish me even more. Storm made sure I was never alone with them the rest of that visit, or on any visit until I was old enough to take care of myself.

The twins were both married now, with families of their own. Travis lived in Austin and Trevor lived in Dallas, so I didn't see them that often. Maybe they'd changed in the intervening years, but I didn't interact with them enough to know for sure.

"Scotty?"

I jumped. I'd been so lost in my head and memories I'd slipped away from the present. "Sorry, Taylor." I swallowed. "I was just remembering a wonderful moment from my childhood when my asshole cousins locked me in an armoire on the fourth floor."

"Travis and Trevor"—Taylor nodded—"Mom's told me all about them." The tone of his voice made it clear her intense dislike of the twins came through loud and clear. Like Colin and Frank, Taylor had taken to calling my mother Mom, which she loved and so did I. She'd basically adopted all three of them. I wasn't sure how his birth mother felt about that but didn't much care. I could tolerate her, but I hadn't forgiven her for how awful she'd treated him when he came out. She'd left his father and moved to New Orleans to try to make things up with Taylor, but I was taking longer to thaw than he was.

Well, she wasn't *my* mother, thank God. Taylor was also more forgiving than I was.

"They're not so bad now that they've grown up, but they were monsters as kids," I said and gasped. "And they loved making me miserable. Never really understood what that was about..."

"You think they knew you were gay?"

"Either that or they just hated me on sight." I shrugged. "After they locked me in the armoire, Storm and Rain never left me alone with them again." I shook my head. "I don't interact with them much anymore, but I'd like to think they've matured."

"Mom says it's too late for them."

"Well, you know how Mom is. They were mean to me, so she'll always think they're horrible." I smothered a grin. "Me, I am a bit more optimistic than that. People can grow and change, you know."

"Yeah, but they have to want to, don't they?" He got a faraway look on his face. I wondered if he was thinking about his father.

I know I hit the lottery with my parents.

I've always been grateful I was born to them and not some horrible couple whose minds had been twisted by hate and religion. Both Frank and Taylor were born into those kinds of families—and not just them. So many queer kids were rejected by their parents or were so afraid of being cut off they stayed miserable in their closets. Or they killed themselves—those numbers were staggering and heartbreaking. Nothing made me sadder than knowing parents, the people who were supposed to *always* love you and want the best for you, could cut off their children over something they couldn't help—no one could help who they were attracted to and who they weren't. Mom and Dad called them unnatural parents, who only had children as props for their so-called picture-perfect nuclear family bullshit. Mom felt like those people shouldn't be allowed to parent in the first place. Knowing his parents had tossed him out like garbage drove Mom to enfold Taylor within her protective wings and pull out her flaming sword. I felt that way, too, and the fact he looked so much like Frank…I sometimes thought of him as ours. People always mistook him and Frank for father and son.

And I love my little queer family.

I couldn't imagine my parents ever having me kidnapped and sending me to gay conversion therapy camp. That's what Taylor's dad tried with him last Christmas.

We found Taylor and put a stop to it.

Taylor's dad was lucky Mom never got her hands on him.

I'm still not sure we shouldn't have let her.

I was just about to say something when there was another loud thump from the fourth floor. I turned from Taylor to head up when he said, again, "It's just Gabe and Vangie." He was insistent. "You don't need to go up there, they're just playing."

"Taylor—" I turned back to him, almost losing my balance, and had to grab the railing. My phone fell out of my hand, bounced and skittered across the carpet, the flashlight strobing as it bounced repeatedly and came to rest with the light facing up…

And illuminating the curious faces of Gabe and Vangie, who had silently come down the hallway behind Taylor while we were talking.

"I don't see how they could have made that noise when they're right here," I said drily, holding out my hand. "Do you mind picking up my phone?"

I could see he was blushing in the dim light.

"Wait a minute, why don't you want me to go up there?" I raised an eyebrow. "We're in the middle of a big storm, Taylor, a dangerous one. Hurricane Lesson 532: If you hear a weird noise inside your house, you've got to check it out. It could be something serious."

"I'm not trying—"

"Stop, Taylor," a voice said from above me. "I don't like hiding, anyway."

Startled, I raised my phone to see Brody smiling apologetically down from over the banister on the next flight up. "Brody," I said, my body relaxing and sagging in relief. "I should have known." I turned back to Taylor. "You snuck him in here anyway? Even after we told you no?"

"It's not his fault, Scotty." Brody gracefully descended the stairs, his fingers lightly trailing on the railing. Brody was one of those guys who were too pretty for their own good. Curly black hair, gold-flecked blue eyes, and of course, the body of a ballet dancer. He was wearing a Bourbon Pub muscle shirt over black sweatpants. His feet, battered by years of rehearsing and overextending and the pounding they took with his ballet, were bare and perfectly arched and pointed, like always. He was a little taller than me, and he hadn't showered yet. His mop of curly dark hair was unruly, and he hadn't shaved yet this morning. "I made him. Mom was on duty at the hospital all night and is staying there until the storm is over. I just didn't want to ride it out at home by myself." He held up his calloused hands. "You can understand that, right?" Brody lived in the very same Lower Ninth Ward that flooded during Katrina. I hadn't thought about that when I'd said no originally. That would have been a trump card to my no, for sure.

I groaned. "Taylor, why didn't you just tell me that when you asked me?"

"You said no so fast I didn't see the point." Taylor's voice was sulky.

I rubbed my eyes. "You should have told me. If I'd known Brody was going to be home alone, of course I would have said yes." I kept forgetting Taylor was twenty-one and had been raised differently than me. Mom and Dad were always reasonable, so that was what I was used to and how I tried to be with Taylor. In my family, you never just took no for an answer. And I could admit when I was wrong. "Well, I was worried about Papa and Maman and how they'd feel about the two of you—"

"Maman knows we're having sex." Taylor stuck out his lower lip, folding his arms and giving me a smug look. He looked so much like Frank it was almost painful.

"Well, it's none of my business anyway, and for the record, Maman told me this morning she wished she'd invited Brody to come hang with you during this whole thing."

Taylor's face got smug. "I knew she wouldn't care. I told you."

"Well, you're going to have to go downstairs and let her know you snuck Brody into her house without telling her," I said, taking a bit of pleasure in watching the smugness drain off his face. Maman was kind and loving, but she wasn't a fan of things being kept from her. She adored Taylor, but he was kind of awed by both her and Papa. They could be a bit much. "Or should you tell Papa Diderot instead?"

Papa Diderot hated being lied to even more than Maman, and unlike her, he had a temper he wasn't afraid to lose.

He used to scare me when I was a kid. I avoided him as much as I could until I found out he was proud of me. Not releasing my trust funds had more to do with me flunking out of school than anything else, but I didn't know that until I was almost thirty.

"No, Scotty, please, let me tell Maman instead!"

Ignoring him, I said to Brody, "What were you doing that made those loud noises?"

"I knocked over my suitcase," he admitted. "And the second time I knocked it off from the bed."

Relief that I didn't have to check out the top floor flooded through me. "You're both going to have to talk to the cops at some point"—the smug look faded from Taylor's face—"because someone killed Nurse Kristin last night."

The boys exchanged glances and Taylor said, "Let me guess—you found her body?"

"I did," I replied, feeling my face redden. "The storm blew a branch off that live oak across the street. It hit the house. I went to see what happened, and that's when I found her."

Brody shook his head. "You weren't kidding about your family, were you?"

Taylor leaned down and kissed the top of Brody's head. At six four, Taylor was at least six inches taller than his boyfriend. "Like I told you, never a dull moment with my uncles." He winked at me. "Any clues?"

I shook my head. "No, we're letting the cops handle it this time. Blaine and Venus are here. Venus injured her ankle." I quickly filled them in on everything that had already been going on this morning. "And the storm turned and went back out into the Gulf but has already looped around and is coming back." I shook my head. "And while I know you didn't kill Kristin, Brody, nobody knowing you were here overnight isn't going to look great to them."

Taylor grinned in response. "Gotta admit, I kind of prefer this craziness more than I liked my old boring life." He chuckled. "It can be a bit much sometimes, but I'm glad I moved down here to live with my uncles."

I felt my face coloring and my heart swelling. Taylor wasn't expressive. Frank was the same when we first moved in together, and so I wondered if it was genetic or being raised in a similar way—men didn't show emotions or express their feelings because somehow that's manly.

It's such a trap that so many men are brainwashed into, to the detriment of society and everyone else.

Mom and Dad raised us to be, in her words, *whole humans*—comfortable in our skins and not bigoted. I was so lucky to be born to my parents. Sure, we might have had to bail them out of jail for protesting every now and then, but it was worth it. They taught us to be passionate about what we believed in. They were also unrepentant stoners and always had plenty of the best weed they could find. (They'd been pushing for legalization in Louisiana for decades.)

It was a lot to drop someone into.

Colin was adaptable so it wasn't a problem for him, plus he had that charisma that made people likable. It took Frank some getting used to—the weed thing was hard for him after twenty years as a Fed, but he grew and changed and adapted. There was a lot of that lone wolf thing in him—being closeted for so long to protect his job, on top of the toxic masculinity grooming, made it hard for him to shed that training and be less guarded. But the three of us have been through so much together—as they loved to remind me, I had a knack for tripping over bodies and being kidnapped—there was some of that foxhole bonding thing at play. But watching Frank open up over our years together was awesome. Who would have ever guessed he wanted to be a professional wrestler and made that dream come true?

Taylor was reticent when he first came to live with us, and I'd always wondered what he thought about his new life. He'd been quiet and almost broken when he came to live in New Orleans. His parents had disowned him when he came out to them, and he'd had to drop out of the University of

Alabama. I was more than happy to help him embrace being gay, but I always wondered. Less than a week after he arrived, he was with me when some bad guys kidnapped me and set us both adrift on a boat in the Gulf of Mexico with a live tiger on board. We'd survived that experience, and he'd been peripherally involved in every murder we'd stumbled across since. I thought he liked his new life, but he never said one way or another. Mom and Dad treated Taylor like a newly discovered grandson, and he too had blossomed. After the horrible things that happened to him last Christmas, he'd gone into therapy, and we'd all worried about him. He'd already dealt with so much in his young life, and I was concerned about his future. But he went to therapy, was making good grades, started working out with a trainer I'd hired, and now had a boyfriend. He had a good head on his shoulders. I was so proud of him and loved him so much that sometimes I felt a bit overwhelmed—and to hear him say he was glad to be with us?

Made my day, seriously. Hurricane be damned!

The staircase lit up in colors from the stained-glass window over the landing, and thunder shook the big house. I grabbed the railing as the wind picked up and the rain started lashing the building again.

"Come on," I said, "let's get downstairs."

Chapter Nine

Seven of Swords

Flight from the consequences of a dishonorable act

"Did you interact with Kristin much?" I asked Taylor as we headed down the stairs. "I didn't. I only interacted with her whenever I ran into her when I came up here. I don't know much about her, but she seemed nice."

"I thought you were leaving this for the cops?" Taylor raised an eyebrow. "And she was nice. Always friendly, always polite, always wanted to know how I was doing, you know? I don't know how much she knew about—well, you know." His face colored a bit. He was getting better about what happened last Christmas but wasn't all the way there yet. "I never brought it up, but sometimes it seemed like she did know?"

"Erica probably told her," I said as we crossed the landing between the first and second floors. "Telephone, telegram, tell Erica, is what Mom always says."

Brody giggled. "I never met her," he said. "She was never around when I'd come over."

"I did talk to her almost every day." Taylor frowned. "And it's not like we confided in each other or anything, but you know, we talked." Taylor scratched his head. "She was more interested in me than anything else. Nora said Kristin was nosy like that."

"Did she ever talk about herself?" I asked, thinking back. I'd never said more than good morning to her whenever I'd come up to the main house and saw her, but other than being introduced to her I'd never said more than that. Most non-hurricane mornings, I slept until I woke up, usually much later than that morning. I was not nearly as nocturnal as Mom and Dad, so I was usually up before noon. I rarely came up to the main house, and I'd not stepped a foot inside the dower house since we moved onto the property.

Taylor scratched his head. "No, not really." He frowned, thinking. "She told me once about losing her parents to cancer when she was a kid—she said that's why she became a nurse in the first place. I didn't ask a lot of questions because you could see it made her sad to think about. She said a lot of people in the area she was from got cancer."

Where had Colin said she was from? It was upriver, but I couldn't remember exactly where he'd said. Livingston Parish, maybe? The stretch of river between Baton Rouge and New Orleans is called Cancer Alley for a reason—there are petrochemical plants on both sides of the river all the way down to Orleans Parish. Most of those parishes were very poor and controlled by the corporations who owned the plants, buying law enforcement and judges and legislators so they could continue dumping their toxic waste and killing with cancer a poor, mostly nonwhite population no one cared about. Cancer Alley was an embarrassment to the state, and an ever-present symbolic reminder of just how corrupt Louisiana was and always had been. Cancer Alley plants were the sites of many environmental protests resulting in Mom and Dad being arrested. But profit and plunder before people has been the mantra of Louisiana politicians from statehood on. That's why this beautiful and environmentally diverse state was being swallowed by the sea, while its bountiful resources were plundered, with the profits going out of state as the petrochemical companies bought their way out of everything.

Louisiana politicians have always sold their souls cheaply.

"Cancer Alley?" Brody asked, shuddering. "How awful."

If I wasn't mistaken, some of those plants were in the family trust's portfolio. I'd had my shares in those companies sold off and reinvested in green energy.

It still sickened me to know that part of the family fortune had come from giving poor people cancer.

"Do you remember anything else?"

"Not off the top of my head," Taylor said as we descended to the first floor. "I know she wasn't married or involved with anyone—she called herself an old maid a lot. People are usually killed by someone close to them, right?"

"As a general rule, yes," I replied as the grandfather clock in the hallway started chiming ten o'clock. "But that's not always the case." As I well knew. You should always look at the friends and family—spouses killed each other, parents killed children and vice versa. But you couldn't ignore other possibilities. Cops often developed a theory of a case and only looked for evidence to confirm that theory, the kind of tunnel vision that impedes justice and results all too often in wrongful convictions. Another thing Louisiana was notorious for.

But Blaine and Venus were good cops and could be trusted. When I found my first body, they easily could have run me in, kept me overnight for questioning. It could have worked out bad for me had crooked or incompetent cops caught that case.

"It's so wild that someone killed her," Taylor said. "And how did she wind up out on that sidewalk? You said it looked like she was strangled—"

"There were bruises on her neck and another one on her forehead," I replied, "but that may not be the cause of death."

"If someone choked her to death, they had to get close." This from Brody. "And she would have struggled, right?"

It was a good point, and I was a bit disappointed in myself for not thinking of it. *If* that was the cause of death. The body didn't show evidence of a struggle, but she'd been under that big branch, and I wasn't able to examine her closely. There was also no telling what the storm had already washed away, either.

"What do Venus and Blaine think?" Taylor asked.

"You know they won't share info on an active investigation," I replied automatically. "I just can't figure out how her body wound up in front of—" I broke off suddenly. In all the excitement, I'd forgotten about that clean space around the window, and the loose shutter that had its security rod removed. Someone had been inside the carriage house last night, and Venus and Blaine needed to know. I shivered again at the thought a killer had been inside our house while we were sleeping…Had something woken Frank up early? I tried to remember what he'd said when I'd first gotten up but couldn't remember. My short-term memory was getting worse the older I got.

It was probably the weed.

Before I could say anything, Maman came out of the kitchen, the door swinging behind her. She stopped when she saw us, shook her head, and blinked a few times.

"Maman—" I started, but she swooped down on Brody and wrapped her arms around him in a big hug.

"Oh, I'm so glad to see you! How did you get here in this weather?" She kissed his cheek. "I've been worried sick about you and your mom all alone down there in the Lower Ninth."

"Um…" Brody flushed bright red. "Mom's on duty for the storm and…"

She gave Taylor a knowing look. "You snuck him in last night without telling me?"

Taylor blushed. "Scotty said—"

"Oh, he did, did he?" Maman gave me her most glacial look, the one that made her a feared power in the Ladies Who Lunch circles. It was effective. I wanted the floor to open and swallow me up. "It's *my* house, so ask *me*, not my grandson who doesn't live here." She dismissed me with a wave of her hand. "So let me make it clear right now: Brody, you and your mother are welcome to come ride any storm out here, it's an open invitation." She squeezed him tighter. "Even if you two break up."

You see where Mom and I got it from? It's in our DNA.

Once you're a member of the family, you're always a member of the family.

She stepped back from Brody and looked at Taylor. "Have you two eaten this morning?" She raised an eyebrow at Brody. "And don't tell me you didn't have dinner last night."

"I had a burger last night." He grinned at her. "But I *am* hungry."

"Me too," Taylor added, giving her puppy dog eyes.

"Well, come on, let's go into the kitchen." She let go of Brody and gestured to the kitchen door. "Let's see what we have and what we can do—"

The door swung closed behind them.

She didn't ask me if *I* was hungry.

My stomach growled.

But first, I needed to talk to Venus.

Maman's study was a very small room in the back of the house, tucked away in the back right corner of the first floor. She always said she liked that it was so cozy. (Papa's study was huge, but that was how the house had been designed when it was rebuilt after the fire. The master of the house always had a big study, where he could do his important work and where gentlemen could retire to for brandy and cigars after dinner. The smaller study was for the lady of the house and had been the house's control center since it was finished.) The room had enormous windows rising about eight feet from the floor, with access to both the back and side galleries through them. Heavy pink and white damask drapes, with long brocade ties with tassels, covered the windows. All four walls had built-in bookshelves, overflowing with books.

When I was a kid, I loved using Maman's windows to go outside. It was one of the few rooms in the house where Maman felt she could decorate just for herself, and she had. The walls were covered with white wallpaper with flocked pink roses. There was a matching pink and white Oriental rug she used to cover the shiny hardwood floor. Over the fireplace was an ancient oil painting of the postwar Diderot family, one of the few things rescued when the original house had burned. I'd never liked that painting, just like I'd never liked any of the oil portraits of ancestors, suspended on wires from the crown molding over twelve feet overhead.

The door to Maman's study was open. Some faint light spilled out into the gloomy hallway. All the shutters were closed and bolted, blocking what little natural light there was.

I didn't like that, either. The house was too gloomy and filled with shadows.

And how many ghosts haunted this place?

I rapped lightly on the doorframe with my knuckles. "How you feeling, girl?"

Maman's very comfortable pink and white love seat had been folded out into a bed. Venus was sitting up, propped against the backrest, the shuttered windows behind her. There was a thin blue thermal blanket spread out over her legs, her damaged ankle elevated on a stack of pillows. A carafe of coffee sat on a small side table to her left. Maman's rolltop desk had been pushed up against a bookcase on an interior wall, the one where Maman kept her oversized coffee-table art books from museum giftshops all around the world. Several shelves were devoted to books about various aspects of New Orleans—art, architecture, history. Some were very old and rare.

The Diderots have always been a family that loved books.

"Hey Scotty, come on in," she said, giving me a loopy grin and waving me in. She shook her head slightly. "That pill your housekeeper gave me sure did the trick, but I feel like..." She frowned. "Like my head is hollow? Does that make any sense?

I feel like I can hear air going through my head from ear to ear. I don't much like it, but there's no pain anywhere, and I can see why people get addicted to this." She sighed. "Never realized how many aches and pains I was living with till now." She shook her fist at me but smiled. "I'd slug you if I could. When the call came in about the body, I had a feeling...and when Blaine confirmed the address was your grandparents', I just knew you were involved."

"All I did was find the body," I retorted. "And I barely knew her."

She rolled her eyes and laughed. "How many bodies have you found over the years since that first time I came to take your statement?"

She had a point. We'd met over a dead body, back fifteen years ago on the same Southern Decadence weekend that I'd met Frank and Colin. I didn't want to think about how many there had been since then. I mean, most people never saw a dead body very often, let alone found them. But no matter what that count was now, it's something you never got used to. "More than I'd like to remember," I admitted.

"Just giving you a hard time." She winced a bit as she shifted around in her makeshift bed. "You used to work my last nerve, but I've gotten used to you. And you've helped more than you've hindered—most of the time." She winked. "I sure don't know what y'all are going to do when I finally retire. I'll have to brief my replacement on you three."

"Retire?" My heart sank. This sounded like more than a vague plan for some future time. She didn't look any different than she had fifteen years ago. But it *was* fifteen years that had passed. I'd thought she was in her late thirties or early forties when I first met her and just had always thought of her as that age. I had no idea how old she was. I'd been twenty-nine back then. I didn't look the same, much as I hated to admit it. Still no gray pubic hair, though.

Having Venus on the force had become helpful. She'd

known us long enough to not immediately assume I was a murderer when I came across a body.

But I could never let her find out I'd helped cover up a murder once.

"I've been putting it off for one reason or another long enough," she replied. "I could be hanging out with my grandkids today, instead of riding out a hurricane with a broken ankle and a ruined crime scene." She sighed again. "It must be the painkiller, but Scotty, I don't know that we'll ever find the killer. There's no evidence left at the crime scene, so we've got to hope there's some evidence on her body that can point us in the right direction—and we don't know how long she was out there. No telling what the rain washed away."

"Well, by the time that wears off, you'll be at the emergency room," I replied, sitting down in Maman's rolling desk chair and swiveling around to look at her. "Are you looking forward to retirement?"

"You don't know the half of it." She made another face. "I should have put in for it when I turned sixty. I decided to wait for Social Security and Medicare." She made a fist and knocked herself on the forehead. "I could be living my best life right now, instead of sitting here with a broken ankle, loopy from someone else's pain pills, trying to solve a murder during a hurricane." She cocked her head at me. "I'm kind of surprised you're not trying to catch the killer."

"Well, as you like to remind me, I get lucky a lot," I admitted, figuring she wouldn't remember this conversation later, thanks to the wonders of oxycodone. "What do you think?"

She scratched her head. "It's a shame about the rain," she said after a few seconds. "We can't tell if she was killed there or just dumped. Maybe there's some evidence on her clothes, but we're not going to get that today or maybe not even tomorrow."

"I think she may have been killed in the carriage house,"

I replied, and when she raised her eyebrows, I reminded her about the banging shutter, and shared with her how the area around the window had all been cleaned up. "The rest of the space was dusty and cobwebbed—you know what a storage space in New Orleans looks like after a few months."

She made a face. "But..." She pursed her lips and whistled for a moment. "But if the killer did that, wasn't that a lot of trouble to go to? And what was he covering up, in the first place? And why take the body out the window? There's a door to the street, isn't there? I know I saw another one next to the door to the stairs, right?"

I nodded. "It was just unusual, so I thought I'd bring it up. It doesn't make a lot of sense to me either"—I hadn't made the connections she had, and she was right, but no need to let her know that—"but why would someone want to kill Kristin in the first place?"

"Weird not being able to access the internet," she went on, her eyes starting to droop a little. She jerked back to attention and poured herself another cup of coffee from the carafe. "Pill's making me sleepy."

"Do you want me to let you get some sleep?"

She shook her head. "No, I want to keep my brain active." She shifted again, groaning a bit, and I helped rearrange her pillows so she could sit up more. "But you don't have to stay if I doze off. Blaine's interviewing everyone?"

"Oh, there's someone else in the house we didn't know about." I shook my head. "Taylor snuck his boyfriend in last night to ride it out here. I had already told him no, but he didn't listen, if that's what you're about to ask, and—"

"He still seeing Brody Shepherd?" She leaned her head back and closed her eyes. "The one who was tangled up in your last murder?"

I nodded. "One and the same. Taylor stashed him up on the fourth floor—"

"How many floors?"

"Four, plus the attic," I explained. "The attic is unfinished, just planks on the floors and studs, and a lot of furniture is stored up there. The roofline kind of messes the space up there, so no one's ever bothered with trying to finish it. It's not like this place needs any more rooms."

"I can't imagine the upkeep," she replied. "The Entergy bill alone must be thousands of dollars every month. I know what Blaine and his husband paid for that big old house of theirs"—she'd been renting their carriage house since Katrina—"but people are really attached to these old white elephants."

"I'd sell it, but it won't be mine when Papa and Maman finally go," I replied. "Mom's brother will get it as the only son. He hasn't lived here since before college, and he doesn't seem that interested in living here now. I guess it'll finally be sold to some tech billionaire or movie star or someone like that. The end of an era, but…maybe it's time for that era to end?" I thought about the profits from Cancer Alley and the history of enslavement.

Yeah, like the Confederate statues, things left from that era should be put to bed.

"Maybe. You swear someone had cleaned up the dust in the carriage house? You'd swear to it?"

"Well, I can't swear to when it was done, and I don't know who did it. I didn't spend a lot of time down there, it's just storage." I thought for a moment. "No one should have been in the carriage house at all yesterday. There's a key up here—all the spares are kept up here, of course—so someone could have accessed the keys up here—"

"Doesn't the house have a security system? Every house in the Garden District does, don't they?"

"Yes, and there's also security cameras." I shrugged. "So once those come back online again, after the power comes back, we'll be able to see who dropped off the body, who was around the carriage house that shouldn't have been."

She laughed. "You didn't think to look before the power went out?"

"The cameras all feed to a computer system that records and backs up to the cloud every twelve hours," I said. "But I don't think it's on the generator. Maybe the security company…"

She made a face. "There's a hurricane coming, there's no one at the controls there, Scotty. But that's good to know. Why didn't you say anything sooner?"

"I forgot." I felt my cheeks turning red. "If this was my place, it would have been the first thing I would have done. But between the storm and Kristin's body…"

"We should probably search the house," she mumbled. Her eyes looked droopy. "If Brody snuck in, anyone could have…" Her head lolled off to one side and her eyes closed.

She didn't respond when I said her name, so I tiptoed out of the room and gently closed the door behind me.

As I walked up the hallway, I heard voices from the open door to the den. The den was just another big sitting room, where the ladies went for their after-dinner sherry in the olden days. The walls were covered with green and gold flocked wallpaper, and the heavy wooden furniture matched. Frank and Papa Diderot were playing cribbage. Brody and Taylor were seated at a small round table, eating omelets. "Hey guys," I said, plopping down on a green and gold sofa that was a little too stiff for comfort.

"Well, you know where your aunt and Venus are," Frank said without looking up. "And Blaine's interviewing Nora in the front room."

"There's not been a murder on this property in decades," Papa replied, taking his turn and scowling as it didn't go well.

"I didn't know there ever had been one," I said, pulling a very comfortable wingback chair to where they were playing, and sitting down.

"Diderots have been living on this property since the

mid-1800s," Papa went on. "You already know some of the ghost stories."

"There's more than one?" Frank glanced at Papa, his eyebrows raised. "I just know about the one in the dower house."

"It's all nonsense, of course." Papa took another turn and scored a few more points. "If angry spirits were trapped on earth, they'd be all over this city. We'd bump into 'em everywhere."

"Well, they say every house here is haunted," I replied.

"Tour guide bullshit," Papa scoffed. He'd never been a tall man, but we used to be about the same height when he was younger. He'd shrunk a bit but still looked fit. He'd always been slim, and never put on much weight. His white hair wasn't as thick or full as it used to be, and his face looked like a desertscape, wrinkles and folds and bumps and a few scars. His blue eyes were redder and looked more watery than they used to be, and the wire-rimmed silver glasses perched on the end of his nose were thicker. He was wearing a loose-fitting pair of jeans and an LSU T-shirt, with slippers on his feet. He sipped from a cut crystal glass of ice water. "New Orleans has always had a dark history and has always been a dark city." He put the glass back down carefully on a coaster. No one dared not use a coaster in Maman's house. "But I've never had any experiences, and I've lived here for over ninety years. Not a damned thing."

Papa and Maman had never been told about my gifts, such as they were, because there was never a need. My parents and siblings were the only family members who did know, and most of them thought it was just something else to tease me about—but they always wanted me to read the tarot for them.

And there was no need to tell them about the discomfort I always felt in the house.

"Didn't you think you saw something over at the dower

house this morning?" Frank took his turn, but I could see Papa was going to probably beat him on the next turn.

"What?" Papa turned his attention to me, his thick white eyebrows knitted together. "You saw something?"

"It was probably nothing," I replied, watching him win the rounds. "I thought I saw a light over there a couple of times, but it was probably just my imagination. You really can't see much when the rain is coming down." As the words came out, I realized the rain and wind had died down again. "Any updates on the storm?"

"Last I checked, it was still spinning offshore and starting to head back for landfall," Frank said, picking up his phone and touching the screen. He read something and said, "Yes, it's moving back to the shore…They are predicting it will hit here, at its current speed, in about two hours." He put his phone back down. "I hate this waiting." He shivered.

I exhaled. Two more hours before the worst of it?

Yikes.

"Did you already talk to Blaine?" I asked Papa. "Venus thinks we should search the house." I gestured to Brody. "I mean, it makes sense. If he was here all night and no one knew besides Taylor—"

"Not a bad idea at all." Papa smirked. "And yes, I talked to Blaine. I didn't have anything to tell him. I didn't even know this nurse or anything about her. Your aunt hired her from a service." He clicked his tongue. "Should have just let her mother take care of it so it was done right."

"It's not Erica's fault her nurse was killed," I replied.

"Everything she touches turns into a disaster," Papa said glumly "If I believed in that sort of thing, which I don't, I'd think Erica was born under an unlucky star. But I've never known anyone to have such bad luck as that poor girl."

I smiled to myself. Mom's theory about Erica's bad luck came from a combination of always coming from a place of negativity and thus drawing more to her, plus always having Papa and Maman there to cushion her falls. "She knows she'll get bailed out, so she doesn't have to make good decisions," Mom always said.

Which was funny to me, because closing ranks against the rest of the world might as well be the Diderot family motto.

"Like that stepson of hers—what was his name?" Papa asked. "The one who threw acid in that guy's face?"

"You know, I'd forgotten about that entire mess," Frank said as he reset the cribbage board for another round. "Until you mentioned it this morning."

"Well, it happened in July of 2005," I replied. "A month later we had a lot of other stuff to worry about."

"I've never heard this story," Taylor said.

I took a deep breath.

Erica's third husband had been a widower with a daughter and two sons from his first marriage. Erica's inability to conceive had always eaten away at her, so she took to mothering those two boys with a vengeance even though both were already grown. Riley, the older boy, was a good-looking enough guy, but he was spoiled, entitled, and didn't handle rejection well. I was still filling in at the Pub whenever they were down a go-go boy. His body was already starting to go to seed a bit the way straight guys always do when they pass thirty. He'd been engaged, but it had been years with no wedding date set—and people were beginning to whisper.

I had no idea he was stalking Apollo Poulos until he was arrested that July.

I knew Apollo, but not well. I'd met him one night when I was filling in at the Pub and he was dancing that night, too. Beauty like Apollo's should be against the law. He was flawless. There wasn't an ounce of anything other than bone and defined muscle on his perfectly proportioned body. His skin was olive and beautiful, and he had the sexiest legs and ass I'd seen at that time. Apollo was kind and nice because he'd floated through life being beautiful and getting treated specially. I was no slouch in my twenties, but nobody noticed me dancing next to him. All I got was his overflow that night. I was attracted to him—everyone was. But as it turned out, he had a client after he got off work that night—he not only was a dancer and a mode, but was also a highly paid escort.

Riley Foster, it turned out, had hired him one night and kept hiring him, eventually getting so obsessed and possessive that Apollo refused to book him anymore. That's when the stalking truly got out of hand. Apollo tried to get a restraining order, but the courts didn't care about protecting a gay nobody from the scion of one of the city's society families.

It was just gay shit, after all. What could go wrong?

Apollo fell in love with a photographer with a gallery on Magazine, and they were planning on moving in together when Riley found out and lost his mind. He went to Apollo's apartment, and when Apollo answered the door, he threw acid in his face.

Apollo was no longer pretty. His face was so damaged it couldn't be repaired completely, leaving him with a frozen face that barely moved, and he'd been blinded in one eye. His nose had to be completely reconstructed. He had been flown to Houston for treatment and care, so he wasn't here when Katrina came in.

Riley was arrested, charged, and released on bail…and in the commotion after Katrina, he disappeared. Later, when things were slowly starting to come back together and the criminal justice system was back to order, the cops found that he'd used his passport to go to France, where he'd simply vanished. I personally always thought Erica had helped him escape and was sending him money wherever he was even after his father divorced her—he divorced her because he also believed she'd helped his son escape justice.

The statute of limitations on the original charges had run out—he'd only been charged with assault—and rumors were rife that his father was trying to buy him a presidential pardon.

I wouldn't come back if I was Riley, but I would have never thrown acid in someone's face, either.

"That's horrible," Brody said, his face pale. "So he got away with ruining Apollo's face?"

"Riley's dad settled with him and he got a lot of money," I replied. "But how much money is your face worth?"

As if in answer to my question, Blaine entered the den, doing a double take when he saw Brody. When I explained how he'd wound up there, Blaine crooked his index finger at him. "Well, intruder, I'll talk to you next."

CHAPTER TEN
TEN OF CUPS
A family quarrel

I followed them out of the den, stomach still growling, so I headed down the hall to the kitchen. Nora was washing dishes in the sink and didn't hear me come in.

It was dark outside, but the wind and rain had lessened. I walked over to the island and grabbed a banana from the fruit bowl. I was unpeeling it when Nora turned off the water and said, "Ah, are you hungry?"

"A little bit, but no need to fuss over me. I can find something myself," I replied before biting the banana.

"I can make you a grilled cheese," she replied. "I picked up Creole tomatoes this week."

"Yes, please." I would have said no—hurricane weather meant regular rules didn't apply, no matter how much Nora hated having other people use the kitchen—but she made the *best* grilled cheese sandwiches. She used bacon, guacamole, and a slice of tomato. And Creole tomatoes were the best tomatoes. I grabbed a Coke out of the refrigerator and hopped up on a barstool at the island as she buttered a cast-iron skillet and two pieces of bread. "How'd it go with Blaine?"

She placed a piece of bread in the skillet. "Okay, I guess. I didn't really have any answers for him."

"How well did you know Kristin?" I asked, taking a swig of Coke and trying not to burp.

"Well enough to recommend her to your aunt," she replied, slicing a thick piece off a tomato. "I met her on my previous job."

"You worked at a plantation home, right, before Maman hired you?"

She nodded. "I worked at Chambord." Chambord wasn't one of the more famous plantations of Louisiana, but it was well known enough.

"Is that close to Baton Rouge?"

She nodded. "Yes, in Livingston Parish."

Kristin had been from Livingston Parish. "And Kristin also worked at Chambord?"

Nora nodded, her face blank, as she reheated two pieces of bacon from the rasher in the microwave. "Yes, she worked for the owner's disabled mother. Mrs. Gentry seemed to like her a lot, and she passed last year. I still had Kristin's number, so when your aunt needed a home care nurse, I thought of her." She took the toasted piece of bread out of the skillet and placed another one down. She layered the bacon, tomato, and cheese on the bread in the skillet before spreading guacamole on the other and laying it on top. "The detective wanted a copy of her résumé, so I got it for him."

And of course, Nora's recommendation ensured Kristin would get the job. Interesting.

But it didn't mean anything, did it? That's how people got jobs all the time—someone knew someone who knew someone. New Orleans had always operated that way. Did it mean something that they'd known each other before working here?

Probably not.

But there was something in my head, nagging at me. Livingston Parish.

I was forgetting something.

Hadn't someone said Kristin's parents died from cancer? And she was from Cancer Alley?

Was Livingston Parish on the river? I wasn't sure, but I didn't think so.

I took a bite from the grilled cheese, which was incredible as always. The guacamole was a little hotter than usual, but it worked. I swallowed. "Thanks, Nora. This is delicious."

She acknowledged me with a slight nod of her head as she wiped out the skillet with a paper towel. Who had told me she was from Cancer Alley? I tried to remember as I finished the grilled cheese sandwich. I sighed. I couldn't think clearly in this house. I put my dish in the sink, thanked Nora again, and walked out into the hallway. I dug my phone out of my pocket and looked at the screen. There was a wireless signal somehow. I opened my browser and typed *Livingston Parish map* into the search bar as I sat down in a wingback chair near the foot of the stairs.

I hadn't considered the possibility that someone in the house had killed Kristin because why would I? It was just my family and Nora. Nora had worked for my family for years now, lived in the house, and was a trusted employee. Why would I suspect her?

Just because I hadn't known she'd referred Kristin to my aunt and had worked with her before didn't mean she had a reason to kill her. And if she did, why wait until the night before a hurricane?

It was possible someone else was in the house. No one had known Brody had been here overnight. Venus was right, we needed to search the house. Just to be safe. Whoever had killed Kristin was long gone by now, but better to know for sure.

There was another roar of thunder, and the wind was rattling the windows on the landing, roaring as it blasted around the big house. I gritted my teeth and closed my eyes. Rain was battering the house again. It had gotten even darker.

And then the wind slowed. It was still blowing, but it didn't sound as angry. The rain picked up, though, the big heavy drops hitting the house like bullets from an automatic weapon, the steady *rat-tat-tat* that usually lulled me to sleep now sounding homicidal. I shivered and wished I had a blanket, that I was curled up in bed with Frank's and Colin's warm bodies on either side of me, snuggled and safe and warm from the fury of thc storm.

An alert popped up on my phone's face: *Hurricane eye approaching landfall along Barataria Bay.*

Barataria Bay was Grand Isle. The eye could miss New Orleans.

The browser was still trying to load a response to my search.

In a pause in the rain, I momentarily heard the clacking of billiard balls before the rain picked up again. The billiard table was in the game room, across the big main hall from the library. I was curious to see who was playing, and if I could recruit them to help search the house. I knew Frank and Papa were in the den playing cribbage. Taylor and Brody were also in the den. I walked across the big main hallway. Another wind gust buffeted the house, shrieking loud enough to wake the dead. I could hear the house straining against the wind, fighting it, determined to stay anchored.

I swallowed. I really hated hurricanes.

The double doors to the game room were open, with some dim light spilling out. The generator primarily kept the key appliances and the air-conditioning on the first floor going. Only some of the lights came back on when the generator kicked in when the power went down.

If powering a building of this size cost a fortune, one of the benefits was all the room. There was always room to put up people if needed. Relatives were always put up here for weddings and other occasions when the whole extended family was invited. Our family tree had so many branches I couldn't begin to keep track of them all. Maman kept track for everyone else, and now she was training my sister to take over from her. It was cool that all these enormous rooms on the first floor were stuffed to overflowing with antiques and gimcracks from all over the world. The house had been renovated and redecorated, restyled and repaired so many times over the years that the family had accumulated a vast amount of furniture. The attic was crammed full of furniture, and so was the first floor of the carriage house. I think they even rented a storage place, too. Papa and Maman were always trying to foist off furniture on all of us. My apartment was full of their castoffs. Mom always thought the house too cluttered, stuffy and stale. If she had a hand in redecorating at some point, Mom would get rid of all this big heavy furniture and the dark rugs and drapes to create open, airy space with lots of light that would be a lot more welcoming.

I still couldn't imagine Mom growing up in this house. Her spirit must have felt so stifled here.

I know mine would have been.

When we were kids, I always imagined the Diderot House when we were playing Clue. It had the right kind of spooky atmosphere. Hell, there even used to be a secret passage. The back staircase by the kitchen used to have hidden doors on every floor, including in the kitchen. Maman and Papa had switched out the secret doors for real ones when I was in my teens.

I poked my head in the door. I grinned as my uncle Misha lined up a bank shot. He tapped it carefully with his stick, and it rebounded off the side into a solid orange ball, which fell into the corner pocket. Colin was chalking the tip of his cue.

"Don't mind me," I said when he looked up. "Just wanted to see who was playing pool."

Misha scowled before breaking into his big sunny grin. He waved the cue at me. "Don't let your grandmother know we're playing. I'm tired of her wiping my ass."

"Kicking," Colin said with a smile. "*Wiping* means something else entirely."

Misha beamed as he lined up his next shot. He still made the occasional wrong word choice that was kind of funny. I didn't like teasing him about the way he talked, but he always took it good-naturedly.

Especially considering English was his third language after Russian and French.

Misha was almost six feet tall and his body was thick and strong and muscular. He could crack walnuts with his pecs. He always wore baggy, shapeless clothes that hid his muscles and had the personality of a teddy bear. He tapped the cue ball, and it ricocheted around the table and kissed the green ball, but the green hit the hole too far to the right and so spun to a rest right at the rim.

"You been filled in?" I asked him as he picked up a glass of wine and sipped from it.

He nodded. "Colin told me about Nurse Kristin. Shame."

"Venus was thinking we might want to search the rest of the house." I told them how Taylor had snuck Brody in for the night, and Venus thought the killer could be inside the house.

"Because they were in the carriage house last night?" Colin asked.

Misha looked confused, so I told him about the cleaned-up area around the loose shutter. He nodded. "So might be in house. Makes sense."

"When did you come by yesterday, Misha?"

Colin sank another ball and was lining up the eight ball. He tapped his cue stick into the far-right pocket. He took the shot, and the ball dropped.

"Enough," Misha said, holding up his hands in defeat. He hung up his pool cue and looked back at me. "I came by Thursday night, when the storm formed out there." He gestured to the south. "I don't like storms."

"I don't think anybody likes them," Colin replied, putting away his cue stick. "Did you get to know Nurse Kristin very well since she came to work here?"

"I come by a lot," he admitted. He hadn't had a father for most of his life, so I couldn't blame him for wanting to spend as much time as he could with Papa. "She seemed nice, but..."

"But?" I prompted.

He screwed up his face. "I don't like to say bad things about dead people, but she did not like Papa. At all."

"Why do you say that?" I asked, retrieving balls from the pockets and rolling them to Colin, who was racking them all. "Did she say something?"

"Nah." He shook his head. "It was just the way she looked when someone said his name, and she always left the room after he would come in." He scratched his head. "Once Papa and I were drinking tea on the back gallery, and I saw her in the window of that little house, staring at Papa, and the look she had on her face..." He shuddered. "I don't want no one to ever look at me like that."

I didn't like the sound of that.

My phone dinged, and I pulled it out of my pocket. The search results had finally loaded, and what I wanted—the map—was right there at the top. I made the picture bigger with my fingers, and yes, I was correct. Livingston Parish was just east of Baton Rouge but didn't reach the Mississippi River.

"Colin, didn't you tell me Kristin was from Cancer Alley?"

He smiled at me. "Yes, she told me that. Her parents died from cancer."

I moved the map around a bit. Yes, Livingston Parish included part of the Manchac Swamp and Lake Maurepas. Was Cancer Alley precisely defined? Poisonous chemical plants were everywhere in Louisiana, and the incidence of cancer in southern Louisiana was at insane levels.

And then it hit me, like a hammer to my head.

Livingston Parish was home to a chemical plant whose parent company the trust was invested in. And I'd asked my part of the trust to sell off any shares I owned.

Because that plant, along with several others, was

responsible for Devil's Swamp Lake, a Superfund site that still hadn't been cleaned up.

Her parents had both died from cancer.

I felt sick to my stomach.

I sat down hard in an armchair, staring at the racked billiard balls on the green felt.

That note in her hand—maybe it wasn't *hill* written on it, maybe it was *all*.

The rain had made the rest of it illegible, so maybe the word I'd read had smeared?

I started scrolling down the results page.

An entire town had to move, and a lot of its residents had gotten cancer. Many had died.

Frenchmen's Bend.

That was the name of the town. It had briefly even made the national news, maybe ten years ago?

Of all times to have slow internet.

Mom.

I knew about Frenchmen's Bend because Mom had done a lot of charity work for the residents when the government shut down the area and moved them out of their homes. Their buyout was a joke, so Mom had worked hard, raising awareness and raising money in New Orleans. I'd written her a big check, and I knew she'd worked with them on finding new places to live and getting settled and dealing with the health issues proximity to that plant had caused. I'd thought it was just another one of Mom's causes, an injustice she wanted to right. Had she known we'd all made money from that plant?

Were *we* responsible for what happened to those poor people?

So my family gave people cancer now. Guess that was a step up from *enslaving* them.

"Are you okay?" Colin whispered, sitting down on the arm of the chair. Startled, I looked up to see we were alone in the room. "I asked Misha to round up some more searchers. You look like you've seen a ghost."

"Worse," I replied hoarsely. How do I explain this to him? To Frank? To Taylor?

Oh, my Lord, *Taylor*.

We were exactly the kind of people he wanted to fight against when he got out of college.

"I think," I whispered, "I have a theory. It's crazy but..."

I was cut off by the arrival of Frank, Taylor, and Brody, followed by Misha. He beamed at me. "Plenty of searchers!"

"We should have already done this," Frank said, giving me a funny look. "Scotty, why don't you and I pair off. Brody, you go with Misha, and Colin, you and Taylor. We'll take the third floor."

Misha had been even more efficient than I'd expected. He started handing out flashlights to everyone out of a sack he'd been carrying and then gave each of us a bottled water. "It's hot and stuffy upstairs," he explained, before leading Brody, Colin, and Taylor to the main staircase.

"We'll take the back stairs," Frank said, pulling me down the hall to the kitchen door. There was no one in the kitchen. I glanced out the back door and stopped short. Frank turned back to me. "Are you okay? You looked like you were about to puke in the game room, and—"

"It's starting to come together for me," I replied, still staring out the back door. "But do you see *that*?"

Frank turned his head. His eyes widened. "Is that a light over at the dower house?"

Relief flooded through me. "You see it, too?"

He nodded. "I believed you before, you know. Someone's over there, and we should probably check it out. And I think maybe we should take a gun with us."

"And get raincoats," I said. He nodded and went out the swinging door. I walked over to the back door and pressed my face against the glass. It had gotten very dark outside, not quite dark as night but close enough. The light showing through the glass, on the inside, was moving. The dower house had been empty last night. Kristin knew that. She also had a key. There had to be a connection between whoever was over there now and her murder. I opened the door a crack, and the wind almost took it out of my hands. The light was gone now—either turned off, or the person had moved out of the window's sight line. The rain was coming down in torrents now, water cascading from the waterspouts and off the sides of the roof. All the paved area around the swimming pool was underwater, which meant the lawn was also under water that wasn't draining off fast enough. My guess was there was water on the first level of the carriage house now.

Good thing Kristin's body got taken off to the morgue, I thought, or she might have just floated down Chestnut Street and who knew where she'd wind up?

"What are you doing?"

"I saw a light over in the dower house," I replied to Nora, not turning around. "Frank saw it, too. He went to get coats so we can go check it out."

"You can't go out there now," Nora replied, washing her hands in the sink. "Just wait a few minutes. This band will pass. And if there's someone over there, they ain't going anywhere."

The light hadn't come back, so I looked over at Nora. "Nora, do you remember what town Kristin was from?"

"Denham Springs." She didn't hesitate. "Why?"

"Are you sure it wasn't Frenchmen's Bend?"

Her face was expressionless. "She never mentioned it. Frenchmen's Bend is that town that got poisoned, isn't it? I was working at Chambord when that happened. Damned shame what those companies did to those people."

If she knew my family was involved, she wasn't going to tell me.

"Why do you ask?" she asked, as Frank swung the door

open, carrying two full-length raincoats and two pairs of rubber boots. If he had a gun, he was hiding it.

"Well, you said you'd met her when you both worked in Livingston Parish, and she told Taylor that her parents died from cancer—"

"She told me that, too."

"So, I just wondered if she was originally from Frenchmen's Bend." I shrugged, taking a pair of boots and a coat from Frank. I slipped my arms into the coat, which was too big for me but would have to do. It reached down past my knees, and I pushed the sleeves up so my hands were free. I belted it and dropped the hood over my head, and pulled the boots on one by one. "What did it say on her résumé?"

"I don't remember anything about Frenchmen's Bend in it," Nora replied. "Maybe she was from there. If she was, she never mentioned it to me."

Frank opened the back door.

"I still think you should wait," she said tonelessly. "It's dangerous out there. Why don't you let Detective Tujague go? Isn't it his job?"

I stopped myself from asking why she didn't want us checking out the dower house. I just stared at her when I heard my grandmother's voice calling, "Nora." Nora dropped her eyes and went out through the swinging door.

I took a deep breath, thinking maybe she was right, maybe we should send Blaine instead, but went out the back door. The wind wasn't blowing hard, but Frank still held the door steady, and I had to help him fight the wind to close it again. The wind picked up, sending raindrops stinging into our faces. It was gloomy outside, like the sun had packed up and moved on. I grabbed hold of my hood with one hand to keep it from blowing off my head, bracing myself against the wind and leaning into it. A branch and some palm leaves blew past. Flying debris was going to be the main problem, and the wind and the rain weren't helping. I grabbed hold of one of the columns and held it with my left hand, while my right hand worked to keep the hood on my head. There was so much rain I couldn't really see anything, so I tilted my head down. I could see Frank's boots not far from me—he was holding on to the opposite railing.

I was about to let go and fight my way back to the back door when the wind slowed. The rain was still deluging down, but I didn't have to fight the wind anymore. I stepped down to the first step and grabbed the railing. I almost slipped on the third step but caught myself and finally stepped down off the stairs into three inches of water covering the backyard, but flowing to the lip of the swimming pool. The current was fast, too. I heard Frank clunking down the stairs and started walking through the water. My quads and calves started aching quickly, so I stopped picking my feet up and shuffled through the water. That was easier and got me moving faster, which was great. The wind picked up as I walked alongside the pool, whose water level was rising faster and faster. I picked my head up to see if I could see any light at the dower house, but too much rain was coming down far too quickly for much visibility. I kept sloshing and shuffling my way to the two steps up to the porch. There wasn't any water on the porch because the ground had a slight rise after the pool—so water could drain down into the pool. I opened the screen door, fighting the wind the whole way, but Frank came up behind me and grabbed it. He held the door while I unlocked the front door and burst inside, reaching into my pocket for a flashlight as I stood dripping in the foyer.

Frank turned on his light behind me, and the screen door slammed shut.

I flipped on mine and shone it into the main room.

The dower house was exactly that—a home for older women in the family to use if they chose. The main bedroom suite was on the first floor, down a short hallway from the foyer, and took up at least half the first floor. The rest was a small kitchen, a small dining room, and an enormous living room. My light found the stuffed deer heads above the fireplace in the living room, their dead black glass eyes reflecting light back at me. It smelled musty inside, like stale air, like the windows hadn't been opened since Vietnam.

And if there was a ghost over here, I didn't feel anything.

My head felt better over here than it had all day at the main house. That light little buzzing noise was gone, the pressure in my sinuses I'd tried explaining away due to barometric pressure, but those conditions weren't different over here. I walked into the living room and turned my light to the big picture windows. The shutters were closed, but when I shone the flashlight at them, I could see slats were missing.

I'd seen light through the missing slats. One mystery solved.

I couldn't see the main house through the rain and gloom, though.

"What were you saying about Frenchmen's Bend?" Frank whispered.

"You don't have to whisper," I said in my normal voice. "If someone's here, they had to hear us open the front door. And if no one's here, well…"

I could sense him rolling his eyes. "Frenchmen's Bend?"

I took a deep breath. "Remember a couple of years ago when Taylor was shaming us about the Confederate monuments?" He'd dragged us for filth, wondering why we'd thought they were okay before. And we had to admit we'd never given it a thought. I mean, I did. I hated calling it Lee Circle (I used to call it *politically incorrect Lee Circle*), and the rest of the veneration of the Lost Cause around the city had never sat right with me, but I never did anything about it.

"Uh-huh."

"Well, that was when I decided to check out what my trust was invested in—it was all pretty much the same things everyone else is, but when I saw that we were invested in

Atwater Biochemical, I had the money pulled out of every company that was destroying the world and moved it all into green energy." It still felt like a pathetic response, dripping with privilege. "Well, Atwater was one of those companies that poisoned that Superfund site in Livingston Parish. The town was Frenchmen's Bend. Kristin's parents died from cancer. She was from Livingston Parish. Nora says she doesn't know if Kristin was from there—"

"Nora?"

"Nora was the one who recommended Kristin to Erica. They'd worked together at Chambord, in Livingston Parish."

"And Kristin knew the dower house would be empty, and she had keys," Frank went on. "But who killed her?"

"I don't know," I replied. "I didn't see if her car was parked here, did you?"

"Too dark and rainy to see," Frank said.

"It's a reach, but I think Kristin came to work here with an agenda." I went on, turning the flashlight around the room.

"It's a lot of ifs," Frank replied, moving to the hallway. He shone his light into the dining room—nothing—and there was no one in either the kitchen or the main bedroom. The main bedroom was filled with dying flowers, their fermenting smell nauseating and cloying. The bed was made, and on the bedside table Erica had set up framed photographs. One was Papa and Maman, at their sixtieth wedding anniversary. I shouldn't have been surprised that the other one was of Riley Foster. I shook my head. Why was she so obsessed with that criminal? I could also smell a heavy dose of Erica's perfume (she only wore Chanel No. 5) under the rot of the flowers. There was a notepad next to the phone on her nightstand.

I shone my light on it. The notepad was blank, and I didn't see any ghost writing on it.

I walked over to one of the windows. I raised it and unlatched the shutters. This side of the house was out of the wind. I shone my light at the cars in the parking area. There was Papa's Mercedes, Maman's white Lexus, Nora's Honda... and Kristin's Kia.

"Kristin's car is here," I said over the wind and the rain as I relatched the shutters and closed the window. "Another mystery solved. She must have come back last night after everyone went to bed. But why?"

"Maybe..." Frank's eyebrows knit together over his nose. "Maybe *she* was planning on killing someone. I mean, if your theory is right, maybe she got the job here and that was her plan. Only someone killed her *first*." He laughed. "And who would suspect a nurse?"

She had to be from Frenchmen's Bend, and we can prove it after the storm passes.

But who killed her, and how had she ended up in front of the carriage house?

Frank gestured with his light over to the stairs. I headed up, shining the light ahead of me. The second floor was bedrooms and closets and bathrooms mostly, but once I was almost to the top of the stairs, I almost gagged from the stench.

One thing I do know is the smell of death when I encounter it.

I turned to Frank and held my nose. He nodded to let me know he smelled it, too.

The smell was strongest coming from behind the farthest door down the hallway.

Frank elbowed me out of the way and flung the door open.

I almost vomited. Frank was coughing, but through my watering eyes I could see he was shining the flashlight into the room.

I stood next to him and looked at the body lying face down on the floor. There were some flies buzzing around, and the back of the head was drenched in blood, which was dripping down into a pool on the floor. The bowels had voided, and the smell was ghastly.

The body was wearing a now bloody T-shirt and soiled pair of jeans. There was a wallet in the back pocket.

Frank pulled a pair of tongs out of his coat pocket and grasped the wallet, slowly tugging it out until it was free. He picked it up with the tongs and carried it over to the dusty dresser. Once it was there, he flipped it open.

Inside the window was what appeared to be an Argentine driver's license.

For Riley Foster.

Chapter Eleven

Eight of Wands

Approach to a goal

"Erica has some explaining to do," Frank said grimly.

I nodded, my head spinning. "Let's get out of here—the smell. I just…"

In answer, Frank headed for the doorway. I was right behind him. We picked up speed and galloped down the stairs. Another bright flash of lightning lit up, followed by thunder that lasted a good ten seconds. The wind was picking up again, too. I looked out the window in the front door. It was pouring outside, and the wind was driving the rain sideways. "We're going to have to wait for this band to pass," I said, looking back at Frank. "The full force of the storm is going to be here soon, and if we're still here, we'll be stuck until it's all over."

Frank nodded, his face pale.

I gave him a big hug. "How you doing?"

He kissed the top of my head. "Not great, but…how are you holding up?"

"My stomach is all knotted," I admitted. I didn't want to say out loud that Kristin's murder had helped us both deal with this storm by giving us something else to think about. That was horrible, even if it was true.

And now we had another body.

Frank led me into the living room and we sat down on the big couch facing the big windows. The carriage house apartment's windows didn't have shutters, but it also didn't have any windows facing south, which was where the storms usually came in from. "Do you think Riley might have killed Kristin?"

"Yeah, I do," I replied, thinking. "But who killed Riley? What was he even doing here?" Erica had to know, I realized. Her bedroom suite was downstairs. Riley could have hidden upstairs when Kristin was on duty, or when the night nurse was here. There was no reason for either nurse to go upstairs. He could have been hiding here for weeks, for all we knew. I shuddered. That's the problem with big houses and estates like the Diderot House—all kinds of things can go on without you knowing a thing. "And why was he here? He had other family. Erica wasn't even family anymore."

"But you said they were close, and people suspected her of sending him money after he fled the country, right?"

"His father divorced her a long time ago," I said. "But she could have stayed in touch with Riley." I sighed. "I guess there's no point in trying to figure out any of this, when we can just ask Erica." I shook my head. She hadn't told anyone about Riley being here, even after Kristin was murdered. I had a *lot* of questions for my aunt.

And who killed Riley?

The blood was still fresh, and the body had still been warm.

And I'd seen the mysterious light recently.

But the lights I'd been seeing had been on the *first* floor.

"The killer might still be here," I whispered to Frank. "We didn't check the other bedrooms after finding him."

Frank swallowed and nodded. There was no sound from upstairs, but would we be able to hear it over the storm? He pulled his gun out of his coat pocket and we both stood up. I was sweating inside mine, so I slipped the coat off after grabbing my phone. I grabbed paper towels out of the kitchen to cover our mouths and noses, and a memory of the smell of Vicks VapoRub flashed through my mind. We'd had to smear that under our noses to block the stench of rotting food when we were cleaning out the apartment after Katrina. I thought about checking the bathroom to see if there was any, but probably not. Adults didn't use Vicks, so why would Erica have any?

The paper towels helped some, but not enough. I could feel my gorge rising again as the smell smacked me in the face as I climbed the stairs. When we reached the top of the stairs, we turned right and headed down the hall, avoiding the bedroom with the body. My heart was pounding, my stomach was twisting, burning. I could feel sweat trickling down from my armpits and down the crack of my ass. The bathroom door was open. Frank shone his flashlight in. No one was there, but the bathroom counter wasn't dusty, either. I ran my finger along the surface and checked it. It was clean. But maybe the cleaners did the upstairs every time they came.

Or maybe Riley cleaned it.

The water in the toilet was yellow.

If it's yellow let it mellow, if it's brown flush it down.

The rules for flushing during and after a hurricane.

Frank's eyes met mine over our flashlight beams, and Frank nodded.

The storm was much louder up here on the second floor, and the wind was rattling the windows, shaking the doors, assaulting the roof. I heard a drip and turned my flashlight up toward the ceiling, running it over every inch until I found the wet spot on the ceiling. I shone my beam on it, in time to watch another drop form and fall. There was a weird cracking sound from overhead.

The roof was losing tiles, and the leak would just get worse.

And the ceiling would eventually collapse.

Frank and I moved out of the bathroom and down the hall to the bedroom door on the left. He opened it and swept the room with his flashlight and gun. There was no one in the room. There was a single bed with a white coverlet that matched the drapes. There was a dresser pushed up against a wall, a nightstand next to the bed. The nightstand was bare other than a very old-looking glass lamp. The closet was empty.

But there was a thick layer of dust on top of the dresser.

Maybe the cleaners didn't do the bedrooms? But why would they do the bathroom and not the bedrooms?

The last bedroom was also empty, and just as sterile and utilitarian as the other bedroom. But when I was shining my light around the room, I noticed an irregularity in the outside wall. We're trained in New Orleans to watch for flaws in our walls. Cracks usually mean the wall is going to buckle, which means the foundation shifted, and the sooner that was caught, the less expensive the repair would prove to be. I walked over to the crack, but as I got closer, I recognized it wasn't your usual wall signal of bad, expensive things to come. It was straight, for one thing—cracks rarely made perfect lines—and there was another line across the top at a ninety-degree angle to the one I noticed.

"What the fuck?" Frank asked in his normal voice. "That looks like a door."

"How do we open it?" I asked.

"I'll get a knife from the kitchen," he said and was out the bedroom door in a flash. I heard him clomping down the stairs. I walked over to the window. It was even darker outside than it had been. As I watched, more branches flew past, with the occasional garbage can or lawn chair. I pulled out my phone. No bars, no Wi-Fi signal. Where was the eyewall now? How much longer were we going to have to deal with—

Panic was rising and my mind was about to spiral.

I put both hands against the wall, dropped my head, and focused on breathing in and out. Long slow inhales, long slow exhales. My therapist told me this focus lowered your heart rate, which in turn slowed down the adrenaline response.

As I breathed, I could feel my body calming, slowing down, resting, righting itself.

I heard Frank coming back down the hall. He grinned at me when he walked in carrying a big butcher knife. He stepped over to the outline of the door on the wall. "You didn't know this door was here?"

I shook my head. "No, I had no idea. It's a secret passage, isn't it?"

"The question is, where does it go?" Frank slid the knife blade into the small crack and started moving it upward. Nothing. He started moving down, and when the blade was at about his waist height, there was an audible click and the entire door swung toward us a few inches. Frank grabbed it and pulled it all the way open—and it opened smoothly. I shone my flashlight into the opening to see a moldy brick wall on the other side of some steep stone stairs. There was no railing, but there were footprints in the dust on the stairs. "I hate to go down the stairs and mess up these footprints." Frank frowned.

I pulled out my phone and took some quick pictures of them. "Problem solved." I pointed the flashlight beam down the stairs. They looked like they went down farther than the first floor. It smelled musty, damp and wet inside. I gulped. It was a pretty tight space, but I could see a brick floor at the foot of the steps. They glistened with wetness in my light.

Frank looked down. "You think that goes to the main house?"

I nodded. "Where else would it go? The back stairs from the kitchen used to have hidden doors when I was a kid. But I've never heard anything about another passageway."

"I thought the reason we don't have basements here is because the water table is too high."

"That's true," I replied slowly, thinking. "But there are tunnels in the city. They built one down around where the casino is now, back when they thought about routing I-10 through the French Quarter along the riverfront. And the Diderot House is on a rise. We've never had water in that house from below, or this one, either. So maybe they built one when the dower house was built?" But why? And why have the door in one of the upstairs bedrooms?

We'd probably never know the answer to that question. It must have made sense at the time.

I wasn't sure I wanted to go underground into a tunnel during a hurricane.

Those bricks were *wet*.

How many times had the ground shifted since it was built?

Surely water was already leaking into it.

Would it continue to hold?

The pool was a recent addition. (I think it was put in after the Second World War.) Somehow they'd managed to do it without finding this secret tunnel.

I shook my head. The Diderot family was full of surprises.

Frank started carefully down the stairs, ducking his head in a few places where the ceiling was low. He reached the bottom and gave me a thumbs-up as he pointed his beam down the tunnel. "It looks okay!" he shouted back up to me with a smile. "Come on down!"

I hesitated and swallowed, trying to summon up my nerve.

I wasn't horribly claustrophobic, but I did experience it sometimes. Crowded elevators made me uncomfortable, as did tight spaces. Every possible disaster that could happen to us down there flashed through my mind like some crazy kaleidoscope. The tunnel collapsing, the tunnel flooding, the walls caving in, maybe even meeting the murderer. All these possibilities were still in my mind's eye as I started down the stairs, slowly. I put my hand against the brick wall for balance and pulled it away immediately. The wall bricks were slimy with damp, and the stairs were slippery, too. I was about halfway down when I noticed another door on my right, probably to the first floor living room. I looked back down at my feet and focused on the steps. One, two, three...I was up to thirty by the time I joined Frank at the bottom.

There was enough room for us to stand side by side, barely.

I could feel my heart rate starting to increase again.

Frank's light was swallowed up into darkness down the tunnel. It was narrow—I'd have to walk behind him—and the bricks on the wall and floor were wet and slimy. I could see drops of water coming down from the ceiling in several places. That wasn't a good sign, I thought nervously. An image of the ceiling collapsing, burying Frank and me in mud, bricks, and water flashed through my head, and I could feel sweat beading up all over my body. The air was close and stuffy down there, too.

"Well, here we go," Frank said, but he didn't move. He was going to have to stoop a bit in some places where the ceiling might be too low, but it looked like I could stand up the entire way...as far as I could see, at any rate.

"We don't have to see where this goes," I replied, wiping sweat off my forehead. I was glad we'd taken off our raincoats. "We can just go back upstairs and ride the storm out, go back over once the storm is past."

"No." His tone was reluctant. "We need to get back over there. Dead body upstairs that needs to be reported, remember?"

"It's not like he's going anywhere," I retorted.

Frank looked at me for a moment before laughing. "Come on, let's go." He started walking down the tunnel.

I let him get four steps before I started following him, my nerves clanging and my mind racing. I tried focusing on breathing, counting my steps, anything to free my mind from all the adrenaline and fear racing through my body. I could hear Frank's breathing ahead of me, and at least down here we couldn't hear the storm.

Use logic, think the case through.

Erica had been hiding Riley in the dower house all this time. Had Kristin stopped by on her way back last night and surprised him? Anyone capable of throwing acid in someone's face was capable of murder, for sure. The acid could have killed Apollo. The charges Riley didn't face up to had been a joke. Apollo had a motive to kill Riley, too, but Apollo was now a recluse who rarely left his house, let alone during a hurricane, and he couldn't have known Erica was hiding him in the dower house.

Why had she done that? If the statute of limitations had run, and his dad was getting him a presidential pardon, why did he need to hide anywhere? No one remembered—

Hill. Cyndi Hill.

I stopped walking.

Cyndi Hill was the name of Riley's fiancée when he'd attacked Apollo.

I'd forgotten her name.

Maybe the word on that piece of paper Kristin had been holding was Hill, *and it was a name.*

Cyndi Hill also had a motive for wanting Riley dead. His arrest must have been humiliating for her. I tried to remember more about her. I'd met her only once, at the engagement party Erica had thrown for them. She'd been quiet and soft-spoken, very demure and kind. She had dark bluish-black hair that framed her round face, and she had creamy olive skin and the enormous, expressive eyes of a Renaissance Madonna. She'd been wearing a very simple white silk dress. She was small, not even five feet, with fine delicate bones. She was boyishly slim, and she just missed being beautiful. She hadn't been from New Orleans, I did remember that, but I couldn't remember where she was from. She'd met Riley in grad school, and she'd gotten a job here. I'd felt sorry for her—what was wrong with her that she'd want to marry him of all people? It couldn't have been pleasant to find out that your fiancée not only had sex with other men but was so obsessed with one he'd disfigured him.

How did you explain *that* to your friends and family?

I couldn't remember if I'd met any of her family at the engagement party. I'd met her and not given her a second thought afterward until Riley was arrested.

I closed my eyes and remembered back. The engagement party had been here, of course, instead of at the Foster house up near Tulane. That was Erica's doing. She'd rather throw a party in the Garden District instead of Uptown because she thought that was more impressive. There had been a lot of people at that party. I'd pretty much kept to myself, drinking champagne and filling up on finger food before ducking out as soon as I thought it was permissible.

I could believe Riley killed Kristin, but who killed Riley?

No one in the family had a motive for killing him.

That was the thing stumping me, that I couldn't get my mind around.

I was so lost in thought I plowed right into Frank. I hadn't noticed that he'd stopped walking. He slipped on the slick bricks and sat down, hard.

"Sorry!" I said, leaning down to him. "Are you okay?"

He winced. "Well, my tailbone isn't happy with either of us, but nothing's broken." He slowly got back to his feet, putting one hand on the slippery wall to steady himself.

"Why did you stop?"

He gestured ahead. I followed the beam of my flashlight. About thirty feet ahead of us was another staircase. "I think we've walked far enough to be under the main house," he said, cracking his neck and knuckles. "Are you sure no one has ever mentioned this tunnel before?"

I shook my head. "I had no clue it was here. Are you

kidding? If someone had told me there was a tunnel from the main house to the dower house, I'd have spent my entire childhood looking for it. I don't think Papa and Maman know. They would have said something when they put normal doors on the back stairs, you'd think."

"It's not on the floor plans of the house?"

"Well, I've never seen the floor plans." I thought for a moment. "Papa and Maman have never done any structural renovation, as far as I know. Any changes were cosmetic—new paint, new furniture, that sort of thing. And why else would you look at the floor plans?"

"I think Riley killed Kristin," Frank replied. "I think she came back last night and surprised him, and he killed her. Why he was in the carriage house or put her body out on the sidewalk I can't figure out, but he must have had a reason, right?"

"It's not like we can ask him," I retorted. "Can we get out of this shitty tunnel?" It was getting stuffier, and it almost felt like the walls were getting closer. I closed my eyes and breathed. In, out, in, out.

"Yeah, come on." Frank started walking again, taking long steps with his lengthy legs.

I didn't bother trying to keep up. I was sweating again and too busy keeping my panic under control. It seemed to get worse with every step. Left then right then left again, one foot after the other, every journey begins with a single step, right left right, slip on the bricks, keep walking. The ceiling seemed to be dipping lower the farther I went, and I was breathing faster. The walls seemed narrower and closer, the floor more slippery and wet. *Just your imagination* I kept repeating in my brain, and *this too shall pass.* I tried to control my breathing, but the air was stuffy and stale and my panic was rising…

I stopped walking and closed my eyes. *Focus, Scotty, focus,* I reminded myself.

I felt a little better, so I opened my eyes and started

walking again. I swallowed my panic and my nerves. We were almost out of this underground prison. Eyes on the stairs and keep walking.

About halfway to the stairs, the ceiling dipped very low, with enough drops of muddy water falling that it was almost like a small rain. A brick popped out and landed on the floor, breaking into pieces. That wasn't reassuring. There was a loud groan over my head. Panicking, I ducked under the overhang and walked faster, stumbling and almost falling. I had a quick image in my head of me being buried under tons of earth and brick and my breathing was getting faster again and I was aware of every trickle of sweat on my body. My nose started running, and my hands were shaking. I kept going, determined to escape, knowing that I might not get there before my terrified brain snapped and—

I stubbed my toe hard on the bottom step. Hallelujah, I thought, exhaling with relief. Frank was about halfway up the stairs. I stopped, watching him climb while I tried to catch my breath. There was another loud groaning sound from the tunnel, and as I looked back, a few more bricks fell. The ceiling seemed to sag down another few inches.

I need to get the fuck out of here.

I started climbing, ignoring the complaints from my aching legs. I made a mental note to stop skipping leg day at the gym. I looked up. The staircase ended at the ceiling. But there was a big, tarnished metal ring flashing in the beams of our flashlights. When he was close enough, Frank reached up, grabbed hold of the ring, and yanked it down.

Cooler, fresher air washed over me as Frank climbed up through the trap door.

Glad to get out, I followed him up as quickly as I could and took his outstretched hand so he could help pull me out.

I popped up into a small space lit up only by our flashlights.

Frank turned his light around.

Shelves, overflowing with boxed and canned food.

It was the pantry, right off the kitchen.

We were back in the main house.

I washed my face in the sink while Frank grabbed us two bottles of water from the refrigerator.

The cold water felt amazing as I glugged down half the bottle. "Do you think they're still searching the house?" Frank asked.

"I don't know," I replied. "Why don't you go see, and I'll go check in with Venus and Blaine." I made a face. "And then we can go have a little chat with dear old Aunt Erica."

I felt a thousand times better being out of that tunnel. I'd probably have nightmares about it for months. I walked out of the kitchen into the silence of the great hall. The only sounds were the wind and rain. As the grandfather clock started chiming eleven, I walked into Maman's study. Venus was sitting up in her makeshift bed, reading a murder mystery. She looked up at me and raised her eyebrows. Using a bookmark to mark her page as she closed the book, she asked, "Did your search turn up anything?"

"Another dead body," I replied, taking a seat in an armchair. "Riley Foster. It looked pretty recent, honestly." I told her about Frank and me heading over to the dower house after we'd both seen lights over there, and how we found Riley's dead body on the second floor—and the tunnel.

"A secret passageway?" She shook her head. "And two hidden staircases? Is this a Nancy Drew mystery?"

"Anyone who knew about the passage could have been using it to go back and forth between the two houses with no one knowing," I went on. "I wasn't imagining things when I saw lights over there. It must have been Riley—but that last light had to be the killer." And if the killer had concealed the door on the second floor properly, we'd have never found it.

"You have a theory?"

I nodded. "I'm not so sure about who killed Riley, but I

have an idea. I think Kristin came back last night and surprised him in the dower house. He killed her and disposed of her body." I paused. "Lots of people have reasons to kill Riley, but they didn't have access. If no one knew he was here…the only person who knew must have been Aunt Erica. I think she was hiding him over there for some reason—it doesn't make sense to me, but that's my aunt. Why hide him here where one of her nurses, or anybody on the estate, could have run into him?"

Venus sighed. "There's always a reason, even if it's a stupid one. Occam's razor, Scotty. She probably wanted him close at hand. You said they were close?"

"They were." I nodded. "And still are, apparently."

"Blaine didn't turn up anything with the interviews," she went on. "Nobody in your family had a reason to kill Riley?"

"His only connection to the family was through Erica. I never liked him, he was one of those douche bros, always trying to out-masculine everyone. Of course, since he turned out to be bisexual, that was about his own insecurities. Oh!" I rolled my eyes. "That note I found in Kristin's hand? That word was *Hill*, definitely." I explained how I'd remembered Riley's old fiancée's name, Cyndi Hill.

"You think she might have something to do with killing him?" Venus looked up. "Yes, can I help you?"

I turned my head to see Nora standing in the doorway, expressionless. "Yes, Detective, I was wondering if you needed anything—food or drink?"

Venus picked up the carafe on her side table and shook it. "No, I have plenty of coffee, and I'm not hungry, thank you. I'll let you know."

"I'll come back in about an hour," Nora said mechanically. "What about you, Scotty?"

I smiled. She finally used my name! "I'm good, thank you."

"I'll see if anyone else needs anything, thank you." She moved away from the door. I got up and watched her walk down to the great hall.

I turned back to Venus. Had Nora been listening in on us?

She'd been acting kind of strange ever since we saw the light in the dower house.

Well, we weren't having a normal day, either.

"How long has she worked for your grandparents?" Venus asked.

"Helga retired a few years ago, and they hired her right after," I replied. I looked at Venus. "You don't think—"

Venus made a face. "She's the only person here who's not part of your family," she said. "This math just ain't mathing, Scotty."

"She is a member of the family, though," I insisted, but even as I said the words, I realized how hollow they were. I didn't know Nora hardly at all, and not out of her capacity as housekeeper. *Helga* had been a member of the family; Nora wasn't yet.

But she'd been living here and working for several years. Maman and Papa adored her. She was efficient, quiet, and friendly. Maman enthused about how capable Nora was to anyone who would listen. Why would Nora want to kill Riley?

If it wasn't Nora and there wasn't someone hiding in the house, it had to be a member of the family.

The only person with a connection to Riley was Erica.

Maybe she wasn't as immobilized as she wanted everyone to think?

Erica had grown up here. Maybe she found the tunnel and never told anyone. And who would suspect a woman bedridden with a broken hip?

It was possible.

Riley killed Kristin, Erica had killed Riley.

That didn't make sense, either. Why would she have him hole up with her if she meant to kill him?

Maybe she had him hide with her here to give her a chance to kill him.

I wouldn't put it past her. But why, when she'd helped him escape justice all these years? Erica never admitted to being wrong, ever. Her problems were always someone else's fault, never hers.

Why *had* she been so devoted to this one stepson? The other Foster stepson had been much nicer, more polite, kinder. He was married and lived in Monroe now, if I was remembering right.

Maybe…had Erica been in a relationship with him?

Blech.

I opened my mouth but froze when I heard someone start screaming from the front of the house.

"I'll be right back," I said to Venus. She nodded as I headed out to the hallway. I heard heavy footsteps coming down the main staircase. As I hurried into the great hall, I saw Nora running toward Papa's study, where Erica was set up. I saw my grandmother, standing in the doorway, her face pale. She'd stopped screaming but her eyes were wide, her face frozen in horror. There was broken glass and a puddle at her feet. She looked at me and gurgled, unable to speak, but she pointed with her hand.

I followed her pointed index finger. Aunt Erica was lying in her bed and looked asleep, her head lolling to one side, eyes closed. An enormous comforter that hadn't been there before was draped over her.

I didn't see what had spooked Maman into screaming yet, so I stepped past her into the room.

That's when I saw the thin red line of blood running out of Erica's mouth and down the side of her face to her neck. There was a spreading dark red stain on her pillowcase.

"What the—"

"*Stop!*" Blaine commanded from behind me, and I froze in place. I watched him go past me to my aunt's bedside. He touched her neck, then held his hand just over her mouth. He looked back at me and shook his head. He pulled out his phone and started snapping pictures.

I put my arms around my grandmother, and she melted into my embrace. Her body shook with silent sobs. I held her tighter.

He put his phone back away after taking a lot of pictures. He pulled out some rubber gloves from his pants pocket. Carefully he lifted the comforter off Erica's body—

—to reveal the big knife stuck in her chest.

Chapter Twelve
The Sun
Everything hidden is revealed

Maman went limp in my arms. She wasn't heavy—Diderot women were all on the slender side—so I swung her up into my arms and carried her out of the room to the hallway, where I put her down on a love seat before running into the kitchen to get some water and a damp cloth. No one was in the kitchen, and we'd left the pantry door open. The wind was picking up again and the rain was lashing the house.

Poor Aunt Erica.

My eyes welled up with tears and my body began trembling, which didn't make sense. I'd never liked her, so this sudden onset of overwhelming grief was a surprise. I splashed water into my face. I needed to be strong for Maman and Papa. There would be time to grieve for Erica later and process my feelings. As I wrung out the cold wet dishcloth and grabbed a bottle of water out of the refrigerator, I smiled. *That's what my therapist is for!*

Maman's eyes were fluttering when I reached her side. I put the cloth on her forehead and handed her the bottle. "Here you go, Maman," I whispered. "Just have some water and lie here, okay?"

Her eyes brimmed with tears. "Oh, Scotty." She blinked away the tears and took a sip of the water. "Thank you." She took another drink, and as I watched, I could see her pull herself back together into the unflappable grandmother I'd always known. Her spine straightened, her shoulders went back, and her face morphed from sadness to resolution. She exhaled. "Where's Papa? Can you make sure he's okay?" She shook her head. "He loved that girl so much..."

I nodded and got up, aware of the fatigue in my legs. I was exhausted, physically and emotionally. Once this was all finally over, I thought, I was going to sleep for about a week.

Papa's study was empty, other than Blaine and Erica's body. He was seated in an armchair in a corner of the room, looking at the pictures on his phone and taking notes. He looked up at me. "Crime scene, Scotty, you can't be in here until we can get the scene secured and the Lab here to work it." He exhaled. "You've really outdone yourself this time. Two bodies in a hurricane? How will you top this?" His tone was joking, but he looked and sounded tired.

"Actually, it's three bodies," I corrected him. "I guess Frank didn't tell you about Riley Foster in the dower house?"

His face sagged. "Not natural causes?"

"Blow that caved in the back of his head," I replied. "Did the guys finish searching the house for anyone?"

He shook his head. "They didn't find any trace of someone. I can tell by the look on your face you have a theory?"

I nodded and explained how Frank and I had ended up searching the dower house, and everything that had happened until I heard Maman scream. I then went over my theory that Riley had killed Kristin. "I thought I had at least that part figured out," I concluded, "but have no idea who killed *him*. I thought it might be Erica—"

"With the broken hip?"

"She knew more than she'd let on, at any rate," I replied. "Why else would Riley have been around if she wasn't hiding him over there? Do you have any idea how long she's been dead?"

"Body's still warm," Blaine replied. "And you said Riley's was, too?"

"His blood was fresh," I said, gagging a little. "He couldn't have been dead more than an hour."

"And you're sure no one knew about the tunnel?"

"No." I shrugged. "I know *I* didn't know. My thought was Erica knew, but now she's dead—"

"And we can't ask her." Blaine blew out a raspberry. "I think everyone else went to the game room and is waiting to be interrogated. Why don't you go wait with them, while I update Venus?"

"Okay."

He was right. Everyone was in the game room, but no one was playing games. Papa was sitting on a love seat in the far corner of the room, with Taylor beside him. Papa looked broken, and Taylor had his arm around him, patting his knee with his free hand. Papa also seemed to have shrunk a bit, collapsing in on himself. He was taking Erica's murder hard. Parents shouldn't outlive their children, I thought. How many times had I thought that over the years, encountering grieving parents of a murder victim? Taylor's mom had been beside herself with worry when we'd all thought he'd been kidnapped last spring. Hell, how many times had I burned with a thirst for revenge and justice when something happened to him?

Every. Single. Time.

And Mom had to be told. They hadn't been close, but Erica was her only sister.

The entire funeral process would be miserable. I hated family funerals. Maybe I could talk them into having a private service for the immediate family. I didn't think I could face the litany of soft-spoken *sorry for your loss* from black clad crowds at the service. At least the mausoleum service would be private. The Diderots originally had a mausoleum in the old cemetery, St. Louis Number One, but moved to Lafayette Number One a few blocks away once they'd relocated to the Garden District.

Colin and Frank were on the couch opposite the fireplace.

Nora was sitting by herself, looking down at her hands. Brody and Misha were at the poker table, both glumly staring off into space. Maman was sitting at a table, writing on a pad with a determined look on her face. I closed the door behind me.

"So, did anyone find anything in the search?" I asked.

"Nothing," Colin said. "No sign of anyone on the top floor other than Brody, and nothing on the second or third floors, either."

"Frank told us about Riley," Misha said glumly, "and about the tunnel."

"Who was the last person to see Erica alive?" I asked. I hadn't seen her since I'd initially told her about Kristin. I looked at the clock on the mantel. It was almost noon. I had no concept of time anymore. Had I only been awake for five hours? Seriously?

Three bodies in five hours *was* a new record for me.

Not one I wanted to break anytime soon.

"I brought her a tray around ten thirty," Nora said in a monotone, "and made sure she took her pills."

"How did she seem?"

Nora didn't look up. "The same as always, a little hyped up about the murder, a little overexcited, I thought. I brought her a sandwich and some juice to take her pills with."

"And she was still alive when you took the tray?"

Nora nodded. "I went back about ten minutes later and she was finished, asleep. She always falls asleep when she takes her pain pills, they're very strong," she explained. "That was the last time I saw her."

No one else had seen her since then.

"What I don't understand," Misha said, "is who is doing all these killings? The nurse, this guy Riley, Erica…no one is in the house but us."

"We're all family here," Papa said brokenly. "Maybe someone was coming and going through this tunnel Frank told us about."

"You didn't know about it?" I asked.

Papa shook his head. "I had no idea. I'll have that filled in and closed off once this storm is done with us. I don't like the thought of there being another way into my house. And I'll have to put security cameras in the dower house. That's what I get for being cheap about security." He rubbed his eyes and sank back into the love seat, dejected.

"Don't be absurd, darling," Maman said briskly. "There was no reason for us to worry about it, and there's no sense in blaming yourself for it now. It'll be taken care of, that's what matters."

I was watching Nora the whole time. She wasn't reacting to anything said, just sat there, her head down. Everything started clicking into place in my head.

"I've been thinking," I said slowly, crossing my arms and standing in the center of the room. "Nothing makes any sense, right? I haven't been able to think anything through, because I always get stuck. This theory explains one murder, but not the other two. The main problem, I was thinking, was not being able to look anything up online, you know? We've all been spoiled by the internet. Everyone looks everything up online, instead of the way we used to research, right? I realized it when I wanted to see if Livingston Parish was on the river and was stumped without the wireless. Then I remembered to look in an atlas! I've been so focused on not being able to do anything online that I forgot to just talk to everyone and *think.*"

"Livingston Parish?" Papa raised his head. He looked stricken. "Why were you…?" He let his voice trail off.

"Kristin was originally from Livingston Parish. She met Nora when they were both working at Chambord. Nora recommended Kristin to Aunt Erica, which is how she came to work here in the first place. Nora, was she from Frenchmen's Bend?"

Papa made a strangled noise.

"She lived in Denham Springs. I assumed that was where she was from," Nora replied, still looking down at her lap.

"And were you originally from Livingston Parish, too?" I asked.

"No," she answered. "I'm from Redemption Parish. I moved to Livingston when I got the job at Chambord."

I nodded. "Okay, I'm going to go in another direction now. Do I need to fill in anyone on who Riley Foster was, and his relationship to Aunt Erica?"

"I already did that," Frank volunteered.

"For whatever reason, Erica invited Riley to hide out at the dower house. We may not ever know, since they're both dead now. He was hiding out in the upstairs, because I assume the nurses never needed to go upstairs for any reason. The ceiling is leaking, by the way, Papa, over there."

I heard the pocket doors behind me slide open. I looked back over my shoulder at Blaine, who motioned for me to continue.

"So, Erica was hiding Riley over there from everyone, for whatever reason," I continued. "Then Hester started forming, and everyone made the decision to move her up to the main house."

"She didn't want to," Maman said, looking up from her notepad. "Kristin and I had to talk her into it. Now I understand why."

"Why was Kristin here, was the next question." I started pacing. "She didn't want to leave her patient alone, but the decision was made that she'd see if it was okay to drive in, and if no one heard from her she wasn't coming. So how did she end up dead on the sidewalk behind the carriage house? No one heard from her, she wasn't expected. But her car is parked down by the dower house."

"But she left to go home yesterday," Taylor piped up. "I watched her drive off from the back gallery."

"She came back," I went on. "The dower house was

empty, or so she thought. She had keys. There was a hurricane coming. No one would know she was there until after the storm. I don't know what kind of story she prepared to explain why she was there, but she came back. I believe she came back and found Riley, who freaked out and killed her. Riley carried her body down to the sidewalk and dumped her there. I'll bet her purse and her keys are in the dower house."

"But why did she come back?" Colin asked, smiling. He knew what I was going to say.

"Kristin Pitre was born and raised in Frenchmen's Bend, a small town on the edge of a small swamp. Her parents both died of cancer, which was why she became a nurse. So when the news broke a few years ago about how the chemical plants around Devil's Swamp had been dumping carcinogenic toxins, and it was being declared a Superfund site, and everyone in the town had to be relocated, she put two and two together and figured her parents had been poisoned by the companies who owned those plants." I coughed and cleared my throat. "And the majority stakeholder in the worst offender was the Diderot Trust."

If I'd been expecting gasps, I'd have been disappointed. Papa looked miserable, as did Maman. Taylor's face was beet red, while Brody's was pale in shock. Misha, Frank, and Colin all looked surprised.

"I think Kristin came to work here to avenge her friends and family back in Frenchmen's Bend." I exhaled. "And that was why she came back last night. I also think she knew about the tunnel, because I'm guessing that Erica had found it originally, maybe when she was a little girl, and kept the secret to herself all these years. She liked having secrets, it made her feel like she had something over on everyone else—that's what Mom has always said."

"Your mother was right," Maman agreed.

"Whatever she had planned, she wasn't expecting to find anyone at home when she came back. Riley surprised her, and he killed her, carried her body out to the sidewalk, and left her there. We'll never know why he stuck around. Maybe he thought it would be easier to get away in the chaos after the hurricane? But he did stick around and he ended up dead." In a way, it was almost justice. For both Kristin *and* Apollo.

"So who killed him? And Erica?" Frank asked with a sly wink.

"Let's look at this in a new way." I took a drink from my water bottle. "Okay, say Kristin had never come back last night. She'd still be alive, but I do think Riley and Erica would still be dead *because their murders had nothing to do with Kristin's.*"

This time I did get some gasps.

"I had always thought Riley and Erica were weirdly close. They were, almost from the moment she married his father. It never made sense to me, but then I don't tend to assume the worst about people."

"It's a good trait," Maman said, putting her pen down. "Erica and Riley were sleeping together, from before she married his father. I've always wondered if she married his father to get closer to him." She shuddered delicately. "That was why they got divorced, you know. When he found out..." She clucked her tongue. "And of course, he couldn't wait to come tell me what a slut I'd raised." Her voice shook with anger. "I wasn't very ladylike, I'm afraid, when I threw him out of the house." She took her glasses off and wiped at her eyes. "I didn't speak to Erica for a few years. It was so...so *sordid.*" She shuddered again. "How could she?"

"When you separate the murders, it makes it a lot easier," I went on. "Who would want to kill both Erica and Riley? Sure, Apollo had a motive for killing Riley, but how could he have known that Riley was here? No one knew besides Erica. Or so I thought." Everyone was staring at me, except for Nora. I slowly walked over to her chair and looked at her. "We all forget one thing when we talk about Riley and everything that happened that summer before Katrina. *Riley was engaged.*

His engagement party was in this very house! Riley's fiancée was named Cyndi Hill. And when I found Kristin's body this morning, she was holding a crumpled piece of paper in her hand. The ink had mostly washed away or was illegible, except for one word: *hill*." I looked over at Maman. "Does anyone know what happened to Cyndi Hill?"

"She killed herself," Maman replied. "She suffered from depression, and I know she had some medical issues, but after Riley skipped the country, she hanged herself." She frowned. "I think it was Erica who told me? I'm not sure."

"Well, that lets her off the hook," I replied. "But what about her mother?" I turned back to Nora. "We met her at the engagement party that one time. Sure, Riley and Erica probably knew her better—I can't remember her name, honestly, how awful is that, but it has been fourteen years. People change a lot in fourteen years, even to the point that people who knew them don't recognize them."

Nora tilted her head up, a smug look on her face. "Not one of you recognized me," she sneered, her face changing from its usual pleasantness into a ruthless hardness. "Such fucking snobs, all of you. None of you thought my Cyndi was good enough for that monster, did you? You couldn't even be bothered to remember my name! My daughter was too good for that shit!"

"Did you and Kristin—"

"Bah." She cut me off, waving her hand dismissively. "Yeah, we worked together at Chambord. When she told me she was from Frenchmen's Bend, I let her know that the Diderots were the ones making money off poisoning that town. I couldn't believe my luck when the job here came open. After Cyndi died, I took back my maiden name and started using my middle name, Nora. I thought to myself, surely someone would recognize me, but I should have known better. And I got the damned job! It was like God himself was telling me to avenge my daughter...I just had to be patient and wait for my chance. When Erica broke her hip, I recommended Kristin for the job, and when Erica hired her, it was like it was all meant to be. Kristin had no idea what I was planning—she didn't know about Cyndi. There was no need to tell her."

"You wouldn't have to do anything, would you?" I said in an admiring tone, to encourage her to keep talking. "All you had to do was wind up Kristin, and she'd do your dirty work for you. Not even Erica recognized you?"

"Gray hair and thirty pounds and glasses change the appearance more than you'd think," she went on. "She thought there was something familiar about me but couldn't ever place it. I didn't tell her until right before I stabbed her."

I wanted to collapse into a chair in relief. My work was done; she'd confessed to killing Erica in front of all of us. But now I could see that she had a gun in her lap, since she'd raised it and was pointing it at me. I broke out in a cold sweat.

It wasn't the first time I've had a gun pointed at me. It never gets easier. I've been shot, and it's not fun.

She started to stand up, and I backed away. "Not too far." She smiled at me as she cocked the trigger.

"Do you know what Kristin had planned when she came back?" I asked quickly.

"She didn't tell me," Nora sneered. "I saw her headlights when she came back." I remembered her suite was on that side of the house, past the kitchen. "I got up to go see what the hell she was doing—we weren't supposed to do anything until we had a plan, and we hadn't made one yet. I couldn't have her fucking up everything I'd worked so long and hard for, so I went out there to meet her. It was about one in the morning. She went into the dower house, and I followed her. I saw him strangle her right before my eyes."

"You didn't try to stop him?"

Her eyes glittered. "I recognized him. I didn't want to do anything to scare him away! Both him and Erica, both close enough for me to kill easily? So I hid and watched him carry the body down to the carriage house. I waited for him to go back and went down there to move the body. He'd left it in the storage room, near a window. I lifted her back out through the window, closed and latched the shutters, and then cleaned up all the disturbed dust. I dragged her around and left her on the sidewalk. I came back up here, knowing I'd get a chance at Erica and Riley both during the hurricane. He wasn't going anywhere, and I could take the tunnel—"

"How did you know about the tunnel?" I asked.

"Erica told Kristin, Kristin told me." She smirked. "When you started seeing lights over there this morning, I knew you were seeing Riley, and I would have to take care of him before you went over there to look around. He was already dead when you and Frank saw lights and went over there. I still don't know what that could have been, but with Riley dead I knew I had to kill Erica before you figured it all out." She smiled slightly. "Now my Cyndi can rest in peace at last."

She raised the gun to her mouth and pulled the trigger.

Epilogue

We were finally able to move back home the weekend after Labor Day—and not a minute too soon. After everything that happened the day of Hurricane Hester, I couldn't get away from my grandparents' home fast enough.

We didn't have time to process Nora's suicide—or the three murders—before the full force of Hurricane Hester descended on New Orleans. I'm not sure of the timeline. It all was a blur, but I remember Blaine hustling us all out of the game room and into the front parlor as the rain started coming down and the wind began howling and whipping around the house. I sat on a love seat between Frank and Colin, joining hands with them. Papa and Maman were in a far corner, his arms around her, as they grieved for their murdered child. I was exhausted and felt numb, my thoughts spinning wildly around inside my head like…like debris in a tornado. I didn't feel anything, but I kept seeing it again in my brain, Nora holding that gun up to the softness beneath her chin, the loud bang and her head exploding simultaneously, fast as the blink of an eye. My numb mind was trying to cope with it, process it, all while my stomach churned and turned and boiled with the horror.

Once the storm passed, a strange silence descended on the city, and everyone began to dig out from under.

Hester could have been much, much worse than she

had been. Power was out all over the parish and in most of southeastern Louisiana. Some houses had lost their roofs. Trees and wires were down all over New Orleans. Once we thought it was safe and okay to go back outside, we all went out on the front porch. The air was cool and damp, the sky a shocking blue with wisps of clouds gently scattered across its canvas. The yard was covered with downed branches, leaves, and some other debris. One of the palms had come down across the fence, snapping in half and exposing raw wood in the wound. The cars survived, and so had the outbuildings.

We spent a lot of time being interviewed by the police, but the crime scenes were worked, photographed, and evidence bags filled. The morgue removed the bodies, and I recruited Frank, Colin, Taylor, and Brody to help clean up the game room. The wingback Nora had been sitting in was clearly ruined, but maybe the painting that had her blood and brains and skull fragments sprayed across it could be cleaned by a professional art restorer. I would have thrown it out, but my grandparents aren't me.

We were also lucky in that there wasn't much media coverage. The hurricane had wreaked havoc on the parishes below New Orleans, and the North Shore had flooded some from storm surge, so some deaths at a Garden District mansion got lost in the post-storm coverage. There wasn't that much to report on—we knew who the killers were, and the killers were also deceased. If not for the hurricane, it would have been the talk of New Orleans and might even have gone viral. There *was* a good story there, but you had to dig into it to find it. Most didn't want to make enough of an effort and so…the story died.

Or Papa Diderot had thrown some money around to kill it.

I preferred to believe it was the former.

I was glad to learn that the family had divested from the company that had poisoned everyone around Devil's Swamp Lake, and had set up a trust to take care of the medical bills for those impacted. I guess that hadn't been enough for Kristin, but can money ever take the place of a human being? The more I thought about her, the worse I felt for her. I couldn't imagine going through what she did, and I couldn't blame her for hating us, wanting to punish us, to get justice for what my family's greed did to hers.

Most of our wealth was blood money.

But blood money, as Mom liked to say, spent like regular money. It's what you do with it that matters.

Learning to live with the sins of the past, on the other hand, is another story.

The power came back on about three days or so after the hurricane. As the city returned to normal, Maman and Papa started making arrangements for Erica's funeral. They got rid of her hospital bed and equipment and packed up her personal items in the dower house and her condo on St. Charles. The funeral itself was quiet, and family only—excluding ex-husbands. After we returned to their house after the funeral, Papa and Maman gathered us in the parlor and dropped some surprises on us all.

They had decided, it seemed, to move into Erica's condo on St. Charles. It was smaller, they were getting older, and they wouldn't require a live-in housekeeper there. They were a little gun-shy after Nora's betrayal. I don't know if Maman would ever accept that the woman she'd hired, who had lived in Maman's house for several years, had hated the family and wanted revenge so badly she'd patiently waited for an opportunity to come her way.

"None of this would have happened," Mom told me later, "if Erica had been a bit more discerning about whom she married." She wiped a tear away. "She was a bitch, but she was my sister, you know?" She shook her head. "I always wondered..."

"What the deal was with her and Riley?" I finished for her. "I never understood that myself." I'd cried for my aunt.

Like my mother, I'd not liked her very much, but she was my aunt. More than anything else, I felt sorry for her. We'd never know for certain what went wrong in her life, why she was so involved in protecting Riley.

Thank God we'll never know.

We weren't invited to Riley's funeral. We wouldn't have gone anyway.

I did hear, from a mutual friend, that Riley's death had been cathartic for Apollo. He'd been living in fear ever since Riley jumped bail and disappeared, always worried Riley was coming back for him. I made a mental note to wait a few months and then go see Apollo myself. I'd known him back in the day, and I was a bit ashamed I'd never checked on him after what Riley did to him—not once in fourteen years.

Maybe Riley wasn't a blood relation, but I couldn't indict my own family on its questionable past wealth accumulation if I wasn't stepping in to mitigate harm caused by it, either.

I needed to do better, be better.

But the biggest surprise my grandparents had for us after Erica's funeral was their decision to sell the big house.

"It's just too much," Maman said softly, "and has been for a while. This place is just a huge old white elephant that costs the GDP of some small countries to keep going. If nobody wants to buy it, we'll reconsider. But none of our children or grandchildren want to live here, so why keep it?"

After the initial shock wore off, it made the most sense. Why not live in a luxury condo with concierge service and a cleaning service to come in? None of us wanted the place, and the more I learned about the family, the less I wanted anything to do with the symbol of their sordid history.

And I could get used to the idea of there being no Diderots living in the Garden District for the first time in over a hundred and fifty years.

Those last few weeks before we moved back to our home on Decatur Street flew past, it seemed, every brutally hot August day passing into another. When our house was finished, I couldn't believe how gorgeous it was. The exterior hadn't changed at all, of course—no exterior can be changed without dealing with the Vieux Carré Commission. But the display windows on the first floor were new, and the front door to what used to be a business property was now a big picture window. The glass was bulletproof, of course, and the steel door to the walkway back to the courtyard now looked like a normal door…but good luck to anyone trying to break in. The courtyard itself had been power-washed, and the fountain cleaned.

The back staircase was now entirely enclosed, and climate controlled, with big windows at the landings on every floor, with gorgeous views. The first floor was now our own fitness center, with a sauna and steam room. The residential floors were still residential floors, but with the stairs enclosed the formerly outside-facing doors could be left open. We had the second and third floors for us: The second floor, where Millie and Velma used to live, was now our living room, dining room, and kitchen, while we divided the third floor into a massive bedroom suite with an enormous changing room and bathroom. The fourth floor was still Taylor's bachelor's suite, but we'd made the closet bigger and the living room smaller.

We didn't get moved back in for either my birthday or Decadence, but that was okay. There would, hopefully, be more of both in my future.

I also didn't schedule another appointment with my therapist until after we got all moved back in and settled.

I have a lot of things I need to talk to him about.

About the Author

Greg Herren is a New Orleans-based author and editor. He is a co-founder of the Saints and Sinners Literary Festival, which takes place in New Orleans every spring. He is the author of thirty-three novels, including the Lambda Literary Award winning *Murder in the Rue Chartres*, called by the New Orleans Times-Picayune "the most honest depiction of life in post-Katrina New Orleans published thus far." He co-edited *Love, Bourbon Street: Reflections on New Orleans*, which also won the Lambda Literary Award. His young adult novel *Sleeping Angel* won the Moonbeam Gold Medal for Excellence in Young Adult Mystery/Horror, and *Lake Thirteen* won the silver. He co-edited *Night Shadows: Queer Horror*, which was shortlisted for the Shirley Jackson Award.

He has published over fifty short stories in markets as varied as *Ellery Queen's Mystery Magazine* to the critically acclaimed anthology *New Orleans Noir* to various websites, literary magazines, and anthologies. His erotica anthology *FRATSEX* is the all time best selling title for Insightout Books. He has worked as an editor for Bella Books, Harrington Park Press, and now Bold Strokes Books.

A longtime resident of New Orleans, Greg was a fitness columnist and book reviewer for Window Media for over four years, publishing in the LGBT newspapers *IMPACT News*, *Southern Voice*, and *Houston Voice*. He served a term on the Board of Directors for the National Stonewall Democrats, and served on the founding committee of the Louisiana Stonewall Democrats. He is currently employed as a public health researcher for the NO/AIDS Task Force, and served four years on the board of directors for the Mystery Writers of America.

Books Available From Bold Strokes Books

Hurricane Season Hustle by Greg Herren. Scotty must catch the killer to protect his nearest and dearest, before they strike again. (978-1-63679-882-0)

A Marvelous Murder by David S. Pederson. When a hated director is found dead in his locked study, movie star Victor Marvel, his boyfriend Griff, and friend Eve seek to uncover what really happened to Orland Orcott. (978-1-63679-798-4)

Fatal Foul Play by David S. Pederson. After eight friends are stranded in an old lodge by a blinding snowstorm, a brutal murder leaves Mark Maddox to solve the crime as he discovers deadly secrets about people he thought he knew. (978-1-63679-794-6)

One and Done by Fredrick Smith. One day can lead to a night of passion…and possibly a chance at love. (978-1-63679-564-5)

Puzzles Can Be Deadly by David S. Pederson. Skip loves a good puzzle. Little does he know that a simple phone call will lead him and his boyfriend Henry to the deadliest puzzle he's ever encountered. (978-1-63679-615-4)

Triad Magic by 'Nathan Burgoine. Face-to-face against forces set in motion hundreds of years ago, Luc, Anders, and Curtis—vampire, demon, and wizard—must draw on the power of blood, soul, and magic to stop a killer. (978-1-63679-505-8)

Head Over Heelflip by Sander Santiago. To secure the biggest prizes at the Colorado Amateur Street Sports Tour, Thomas Jefferson will do almost anything, even marrying his best friend and crush—Arturo "Uno" Ortiz. (978-1-63679-489-1)

Mississippi River Mischief by Greg Herren. When a politician turns up dead and Scotty's client is the most obvious suspect, Scotty and his friends set out to prove his client's innocence. (978-1-63679-353-5)

Murder at the Oasis by David S. Pederson. Palm trees, sunshine, and murder await Mason Adler and his friend Walter as they travel from Phoenix to Palm Springs for what was supposed to be a relaxing vacation but ends up being a trip of mystery and intrigue. (978-1-63679-416-7)

The Speed of Slow Changes by Sander Santiago. As Al and Lucas navigate the ups and downs of their polyamorous relationship, only one thing is certain: romance has never been so crowded. (978-1-63679-329-0)

Manny Porter and The Yuletide Murder by D.C. Robeline. Manny only has the holiday season to discover who killed prominent research scientist Phillip Nikolaidis before the judicial system condemns an innocent man to lethal injection. (978-1-63679-313-9)

Corpus Calvin by David Swatling. Cloverkist Inn may be haunted, but a ghost materializes from Jason Dekker's past and Calvin's canine instinct kicks in to protect a young boy from mortal danger. (978-1-62639-428-5)

A Champion for Tinker Creek by D.C. Robeline. Lyle James has rescued his dad's auto repair business, but when city hall condemns his neighborhood, Lyle learns only trusting will save his life and help him find love. (978-1-63679-213-2)

Inherit the Lightning by Bud Gundy. Darcy O'Brien and his sisters learn they are about to inherit an immense fortune, but a family mystery about to unravel after seventy years threatens to destroy everything. (978-1-63679-199-9)

Pursued: Lillian's Story by Felice Picano. Fleeing a disastrous marriage to the Lord Exchequer of England, Lillian of Ravenglass reveals an incident-filled, often bizarre, tale of great wealth and power, perfidy, and betrayal. (978-1-63679-197-5)

Three Left Turns to Nowhere by Jeffrey Ricker, J. Marshall Freeman & 'Nathan Burgoine. Three strangers heading to a convention in Toronto are stranded in rural Ontario, where a small town with a subtle kind of magic leads each to discover what he's been searching for. (978-1-63679-050-3)

One Verse Multi by Sander Santiago. Life was good: promotion, friends, falling in love, discovering that the multi-verse is on a fast track to collision—wait, what? Good thing Martin King works for a company that can fix the problem, right…um…right? (978-1-63679-069-5)

Bold Strokes Books
Quality and Diversity in LGBTQ Literature